AF552233

SLAVES OF SLEEP

L. RON HUBBARD

A DELL BOOK

pains to make such investigation, let them substitute faith for incredulity and receive with honest credence the foregoing legend."

So pleaded Washington Irving for a tale of an enchanted soldier. And in no better words could the case for the following story be presented. As for the seal of Sulayman, look to Kirker's "Cabala Sarracenica." Sulayman—less properly, Solomon—who ruled in Jerusalem about 960 B.C., has left his impression on almost every land, but especially Persia, Arabia and, in general, Africa, where dark tales may be found in moldy books which do not at all agree with the prosaic histories written in modern times. Lord of more than mere men, the treasures he amassed are still rumored to be hidden. His seal is still known in all lands where the black arts flourish and might be said to be the most universal of all magic symbols, probably because of the power Sulayman gained through the use of the original. It consists, properly, of two triangles upon one another to form a six-pointed star which in turn is surrounded by a circle representing fire.

As for *genii*—or, more properly, jinns, jinn, or jan—a very imperfect idea of them is born of the insipid children's translations of "The Arabian Nights Entertainment," but in the original work—which is actually an Arabian history interspersed with legends—the subject is more competently treated. For the ardent researcher, Burton's edition is recommended.

Man is a stubborn creature. He would rather confound himself with "laws" of his own invention than to fatalistically accept perhaps truer but infinitely simpler explanations as offered by the supernatural—though it is a travesty to so group the omnipresent jinn!

And so I commend you to your future nightmares.

L. RON HUBBARD

ONE

It was with a weary frown that Jan Palmer beheld Thompson standing there on the dock. Thompson, like some evil raven, never made his appearance unless to inform Jan in a somehow accusatory way that business, after all, should take precedence over such silly trivialities as sailing. Jan was half minded to put the flattie about and scud back across the wind-patterned Puget Sound; but he had already luffed up into the wind to carry in to the dock, and Thompson had unbent enough to reach for the painter—more as an effort to detain Jan than to help him land.

Jan let go his jib and main halyards and guided the sail down into a restive bundle. He pretended not to notice Thompson, using nearsightedness as his usual excuse—for although nothing was actually wrong with his eyes, he found that glasses helped him in his uneasy maneuvers with mankind.

"The gentleman from the university is here to see you again, Mr. Palmer." Thompson scowled his reproof for such treatment of a man of learning. Everybody but Jan Palmer impressed Thompson. "He has been waiting for more than two hours."

"I wish," said Jan, "you'd tell such people you don't know when I'll be back." He was taking slides from their track, though it was not really necessary for him to unbend his sail in such weather. "I haven't anything to say to him."

"He seems to think differently. It is a shame that

you can't realize the honor such people do you. If your father—"

"Do we have to go into that?" said Jan, fretfully. "I don't like to have to talk to such people. They . . . they make me nervous."

"Your father never had any such difficulties. I told him before he died that it was a mistake—"

"I know," sighed Jan. "It was a mistake. But I didn't ask to be his heir."

"A healthy man rarely leaves a will when he is still young. And you, as his son, should at least have the courtesy to see people when they search you out. It has been a week since you were even near the offices—"

"I've been busy," defended Jan.

"Busy!" said Thompson, pulling his long nose as though to keep from laughing. He had found long, long ago, when Jan was hardly big enough to feed himself, that it was no difficult matter to bully the boy, since there would never be any redress. "Busy with a sailboat when fifteen Alaskan liners are under your control. But you are still keeping the gentleman waiting."

"I'm not going to see him," said Jan in a tone of defiance which already admitted his defeat. "He has no real business with me. It is that model of the Arab dhow. He wants it and I can't part with it, and he'll wheedle and fuss and—" He sat down on the coaming and put his face in his palms. "Oh, why," he wept, "can't people leave me alone?"

"Your father would turn over in his grave if he heard that," said the remorseless Thompson. "There isn't any use of your sitting there like a spoiled child and wailing about people. This gentleman is a professor at the university and he has already looked for you for two hours. As long as you are a Palmer, people will continue to call on you. Now come along."

Resentfully, well knowing he should push this ancient bird of a secretary into his proper position, Jan followed up the path from the beach to the huge, garden-intrenched mansion.

Theoretically the place was his, all his. But that was only theoretically. Actually it was overlorded by a whiskered grandaunt whose already sharp temper had been whetted by the recent injustice of the probate court.

She was waiting now, inside the door, her dark dress stiff with disapproval, her needle-point eyes sighted down her nose, ready to pick up the faint dampness of Jan's footprints.

"Jan! Don't you dare soak that rug with salt water! Indeed! One would think you had been raised on a tide flat for all the regard you have for my efforts to give you a decent home. *Jan!* Don't throw your cap on that table! What would a visitor think?"

"Yes, Aunt Ethel," he replied with resignation. He wished he had nerve enough to say that the house was evidently run for no one but visitors. However, he supposed that he never would. He picked up his cap and gave the rug a wide berth and somehow navigated to the hall which led darkly to his study. At the end, at least, was a sanctuary. Whatever might be said to him in the rest of the house, his own apartment was his castle. The place, in the eyes of all but himself, was such a hideous mess that it dismayed the beholder.

In all truth the place was not really disorderly. It contained a very assorted lot of furniture which Jan, with his father's indulgent permission, had salvaged from the turbulent and dusty seas of the attic. The Palmers, until now, had voyaged the world, and flotsam from many a strange sea had at last been cast up in these rooms. One donor in particular, a cousin who now rested in the deep off Madagascar, had had an eye for oddity, contributing the greater part of the assembled spears and headdresses as well as the truly beautiful blackwood desk all inlaid with pearl and ivory.

This was sanctuary and it irritated Jan to find that he had yet to rid himself of a human being before he could again find any peace.

Professor Frobish raised himself from his chair and bowed deferentially. From his following stretch, it might have been supposed that he had been two whole hours on that cushion. Jan surveyed him without enthusiasm. Indeed, there was only one human being in the world whom Jan granted enthusiastic regard, and she—well—that was wholly impossible. The professor was a vital sort of man, the very sort Jan distrusted the most. It would be impossible to talk such a man down.

"Mr. Palmer, I believe?"

Jan winced at the pressure of the hand and quickly recovered his own. Nervously he wandered around the table and began to pack a pipe.

"Mr. Palmer, I am Frobish, professor of Islamic Culture at the university. I hope you will forgive my intrusion. Indeed, it shows doubtlessly great temerity on my part so to take up the time of one of Seattle's most influential men."

He wants something, Jan told himself. They all want something. He lighted the pipe so as to avoid looking straight at the fellow.

"It has come to our ears that you were fortunate enough to have delivered to you a model—if you'll forgive me for coming to the point, but I know how valuable your time is. This model, I understand, was recovered from a Tunisian ruin and sent to your father—"

He went on and on but Jan was not very attentive. Jan paced restively over to the wide windows and stood contemplating the azure waters backed by the rising green of hills and, finally, by the glory of the shining, snow-capped Olympics. He wished he had been sensible enough to stay out there. Next time he would take his cabin sloop and enough food to last a day or two—but at the same time, realizing the wrath this would bring down upon him, he knew that he would never do so. He turned, puffing hopelessly at his pipe, to watch the Arabic scholar. Suddenly he was struck by the fact that, though the man kept talking about and pointing to the model of the ancient dhow which stood upon the great blackwood desk, his interest did not lie there. On entering the room it might have, but now Frobish's eye kept straying to the darkest corner. What, Jan wondered, in all these trophies had excited this fervid man's greed? Certainly the professor was having a difficult time staying on his subject and wasn't making a very strong case of why the university should be presented with this valuable model.

Jan's schooling, while not flattering to humanity, was nevertheless thorough. His father, too engrossed in shipping to give much time to raising a son, had failed wholly to notice that the household used the boy to bolster up their respective prides which they perforce must humble before the elder Palmer. And since it would not be fitting to give a Palmer a common education, Jan had been deprived of even the solace of youthful companionship. And now, at twenty-seven, he was perfectly aware of the fact that men never did anything without thought of personal gain and that when men reacted strangely they would bear much watching. This professor wanted something besides this innocent dhow.

Jan strolled around the room with seeming aimlessness. Finally, by devious routes, he arrived beside the corner which often caught Frobish's eye. But there was no enlightenment. The only thing there was a rack of Malay swords and a very old copper jar tightly sealed with lead. The krisses were too ordinary; therefore, it must be the jar. But what, pray tell, could an Arabic scholar discover in such a thing? Jan had to think hard—all the while with placid, even timid countenance—to recall the history of the jar.

"And so," Frobish concluded, "you would be doing

science a great favor by at least lending us this model. There is none other like it in existence and it would greatly further our knowledge of the seafaring of the ancient Arabians."

It had been in Jan's mind to say no. But the fellow would stay and argue, he knew. Personally he had rather liked the little dhow with its strangely indestructible rigging.

"I guess you can have it," he said.

Frobish had not expected such an easy victory. But even so he was not greatly elated. He told Jan he was a benefactor of science and put the model into its teak box and then, hesitantly, reached for his hat.

"Thank you so much," he said again. "We'll not be likely to forget this service."

"That's all right," said Jan, wondering why he had given up so easily.

And still the professor lingered on small-talk excuses. At last he ran out of conversation and stood merely fumbling with his hat. Jan scented trouble. He did not know just how or why, but he did.

"This is a very interesting room," said the professor, at last. "Your people must have traveled the Seven Seas a great deal. But then they would have, of course." He gave his hat a hard twist. "Take . . . er . . . take that copper jar, for instance. A very interesting piece of work. Ancient Arabian, also, I presume."

Jan nodded.

"Would it be out of order to ask you where it came from?"

Jan had been remembering and he had the answer ready. And though he suddenly didn't want to talk about that copper jar he heard himself doing so.

"My father's cousin, Greg Palmer, brought it back from the Mediterranean a long time before I was born. He was always bringing things home."

"Interesting," said Frobish. "Must have been quite a fellow."

"Everybody said he wasn't much good," said Jan.

He added ruefully: "I am supposed to be like him, they say. He never held any job for long, but they say he could have been a millionaire a lot of times if he had tried. But he claimed money made a man put his roots down. That's one thing he never did. That's his picture on the wall there."

Frobish inspected it out of policy. "Ah, so? Well, well, I must say that he does look a great deal like you—that is, without your glasses, of course."

"He—" Jan almost said, "He's the only friend I ever had," but he swiftly changed it. "He was very good to me."

"Did . . . ah . . . did he ever say anything about that copper jar?" Frobish could hardly restrain his eagerness.

"Yes," said Jan flatly. "He did. He said it was given to him by a French seiner on the Tunisian coast."

"Is that all?"

"And when he left it here, Aunt Ethel told him it was a heathen thing and that he had to put it in the attic. I used to go up and look at it sometimes and I was pretty curious about it."

"How is that?"

"He made me promise never to open it."

"What! I mean—is that so?" Frobish paced over to it and bent down as though examining it for the first time. "I see that you never did. The seal is still firmly in place."

"I might have if Greg hadn't been killed, but—"

"Ah, yes, I understand. Sentiment." He stood up and sighed. "Well, I must be going. That's a very fine piece of work and I compliment you on your possession of it. Well, good day." But still he didn't leave. He stood with one hand on the doorknob, looking back at the jar. "Ah . . . er . . . have you ever had any curiosity about what it might contain?"

"Of course," said Jan, "but until now I had almost forgotten about it. Ten years ago it was all I could do to keep from looking in it."

"Perhaps you thought about jewels?"

"No . . . not exactly."

Suddenly they both knew what the other was thinking about. But before they could put it into words there came a sharp rap on the door.

Without waiting for an answer, a very officious little man bustled in. He stared hard at Jan and paid no attention whatever to the professor.

"I called three times," he complained.

"I was out on the Sound," said Jan, uneasily.

"There are some papers which have to have your signature," snapped the fellow, throwing a briefcase up on the blackwood desk and pulling the documents out. It was very plain that he resented having to seek Jan out at all.

Jan moved to the desk and picked up a pen. As general manager of the Bering Steamship Corporation, Nathaniel Green had his troubles. And perhaps he had a perfect right to be resentful, having spent all his life in the service of the late Palmer and then having not one share of stock left to him.

"If I could have your power of attorney I wouldn't have to come all the way out here ten and twenty times a day!" said Green. "I have ten thousand things to do and not half enough time to do them in, and yet I have to play messenger boy."

"I'm sorry," said Jan.

"You might at least come down to the office."

Jan shuddered. He had tried that only to have Green browbeat him before clerks and to have dozens of people foisted off on him for interview.

Green swept the papers back into the briefcase and bustled off without another word, as though the entire world of shipping was waiting on his return.

Frobish's face was flushed. He had hardly noticed the character of the interrupter. Now he came to the jar and stood with one hand on it.

"Mr. Palmer, for many years I have been keenly interested in things which—well, which are not exactly open to scientific speculation. It is barely possible that here, under my hand, I have a clue to a problem I have long examined—perhaps I have the answer itself. You do not censure my excitement?"

"You have done research in demonology?"

"As connected with the ancient Egyptians and Arabians. I see that we understand each other perfectly. If this was found in waters off Tunisia, then it is barely possible that it is one of *the* copper jars. You know about them?"

"A little."

"Very few people know much about the jinn. They seem to have vanished from the face of the earth several centuries ago, though there is every reason to suppose that they existed in historical times. Sulayman is said to have converted most of the jinn tribes to the faith of Mohammed after a considerable war. Sulayman was an actual king, and those battles are a part of his court record. This, Mr. Palmer, is not mere decoration on the stopper but the seal of Sulayman!" Frobish was growing very excited. "When several tribes refused to acknowledge Mohammed as the prophet, Sulayman had them thrown into copper jars such as this, stoppered with his seal, and thrown into the sea *off the coast of Tunis!*"

"I know," said Jan, quietly.

"You knew? And yet . . . yet you did not investigate?"

"I gave my word that I would not open that jar."

"Your word. But think, man, what a revelation this would be! Who knows but what this actually contains one of those luckless Ifrits?"

Jan wandered back to his humidor and repacked his pipe. As far as he was concerned the interview was over. He might be bullied into anything, but when it came to breaking his word— Carefully he lighted his pipe.

Frobish's face was feverish. He was straining forward toward Jan, waiting for the acquiescence he felt certain must come. And when at last he found that his own enthusiasm had failed to kindle a return blaze, he threw out his hands in a despairing gesture and marched ahead, forcing Jan back against a chair into which he slumped. Frobish towered over him.

"You can't be human!" cried Frobish. "Don't you understand the importance of this? Have you no personal curiosity whatever? Are you made of wax that you can live for years in the company of a jar which might very well contain the final answer to the age-old question of demonology? For centuries men have maundered on the subject of witches and devils. Recently it became fashionable to deny their existence entirely and to answer all strange phenomena with 'scientific facts' actually no more than bad excuses for learning. Men even deny telepathy in face of all evidence. Once whole civilizations were willing to burn their citizens for witchcraft, but now the reference to devils and goblins brings forth only laughter. But down deep in our hearts, we *know* there is more than a fair possibility that such things exist. And here, man, you have a possible answer!

"If all historical records are correct, then that jar contains an Ifrit. And if it does, think, man, what the jinn could tell us! According to history, they were versed in all the black arts. Today we know nothing of those things. All records died with their last possessors. Most of that knowledge was from hand to hand, father to son. What of the magic of ancient Egypt? What of the mysteries of the India of yesterday? What race in particular was schooled in their usages? The jinn! And here we have one of the jinn, perhaps, entombed in this very room, waiting to express his gratitude upon being released. Do you think for a moment he would fail to give us anything we wanted in the knowledge of the black arts?"

The fragrant fog from his pipe drifted about Jan's head and through it his glasses momentarily flashed. Then he sank back. "If I had not already thought this out, I would have no answer for you. There is no doubt but what the Ifrit—if he is there—has died. Hundreds or thousands of years—"

"Toads have lived in stone longer than that!" cried Frobish. "And toads possess none of the secrets for which science is even now groping. A small matter of suspended animation should create no difficulty for such a being as an Ifrit. You quibble. The point is this: You have here a thing for which I would sell my soul to see, and you put me off. Since the first days in college when I first understood that there were more things in this unvierse than could be answered by a slide rule and a badly conceived physical principle, I have dreamed of such a chance. I tell you, sir, I won't be balked!"

Jan looked questioningly at Frobish. The fellow had suddenly assumed very terrifying proportions. And it was not that Jan distrusted his physical ability so much as his habitual retreat before the face of bullying which made him swallow now.

"I have given my word," he said doggedly. "I know as well as you that that jar may well contain a demon from other ages. But for ten years I slaved to forget it and put it out of my mind forever. And I do not intend to do otherwise now. The only friend I ever had gave me that jar. And now, with Greg Palmer dead, I have no recourse but to keep the promise I gave him. He was at pains to make me understand that I would do myself great harm by breaking that seal, and so I have a double reason to refuse. I could let nothing happen to you in this—"

"My safety is my own responsibility," interrupted Frobish. "If you are afraid to—"

Jan, carried on by the dogged persistence of which he was occasionally capable—though nearly always against other things than man—looked at the floor between his feet and said: "I can say with truth that I am not afraid. I am not master of my own house nor of my slightest possessions; I may be a feather in the hands of others. But there is one thing which I cannot do. I do not want to speak about it any further."

Frobish, finding resistance where he had not thought it possible, backed off, studying the thin, not unhandsome face of his host as though he could find a break in the defenses. But although Jan Palmer wore an expression very close to apology, there was still a set to his jaw which forbade attack. Frobish gave a despairing look at the jar.

"All my life," he said, "I have searched for such a thing. And now I find it here. Here, under the touch of my hands, ready to be opened with the most indifferent methods! And in that jar lies the answer to all my speculations. But you balk me. You barricade the road to truth with a promise given to a dead man. You barricade all my endeavors. From here on I shall never be able to think of anything else but that jar." His voice dropped to a pleading tone. "Can't you see, Mr. Palmer, that I am pleading with you out of the bottom of my heart? Can't you understand what this means to me? You . . . you are rich. You have everything you require—"

"I have nothing. In all things I am a pauper. But in one thing I can hold my own. I cannot and will not break my word. I am sorry. Had you argued so eloquently for this very house you might have had it, because this house is a yoke to me. But you have asked for a thing which is beyond my power to give. I can say nothing more. Please do not come back."

It was a great deal for Jan Palmer to say. Green and Thompson and Aunt Ethel would have been rocked to their very insteps at such a firm stand, had they witnessed it. But Jan Palmer had not been under the thumb of Frobish from the days of his childhood. This concerned nothing but the most private possession a man can have—his honor. And so it was that Frobish ultimately backed out of the door, too agitated even to remember to take the Arabian dhow.

Before Jan closed off the entrance, Frobish had one last glimpse of the copper jar, dull green in the light of the sinking sun. He clamped his mouth shut. He jerked his hat down over his brow. Swiftly he walked away looking not at all like a fellow who has become reconciled to defeat.

Jan had not missed the attitude. Jan had lived too long in the wrong not to know the reactions of men. He had seen his mother hounded to death by relatives. He had felt the resentment toward wealth really meant for his father. He had been through a torturous school and had come out far from unscathed. He knew very definitely that he would see Frobish again. Wearily he closed his door and slumped down in a chair to think.

TWO

Each evening, when the household was assembled at the dining table, Jan Palmer had the feeling that the entire table's attention was devoted to seeing whether or not he would choke on his next mouthful. As long as his father had been alive, this had been the one period of the day when he had been certain of himself. His father had occupied the big chair at the head, filling it amply, and treating one and all to a rough jocosity which was very acceptable—until his father had retired to his study for the night. Then it seemed that his rough jests were not at all lightly received. Quite obvious it had been that fawning was a wearying business at best and that those so engaged were apt to revert at the slightest excuse.

Jan didn't come close to filling the big chair. His slight body could have gone three times between the arms of it. And Aunt Ethel and Thompson and, occasionally as tonight, Nathaniel Green, found no reason whatever to do any fawning.

Having very early deserted the bosom of his family for the flinty chest of Socrates, Jan knew quite well that if he had had the dispensing of funds comparable to those of his father in his entire control, smiles and not scowls would now be his lot. But the Bering Steamship Corporation was not showing much of a profit. Just why he did not know. He had never peeped into the books, but he supposed that these continual strikes had something to do with it. The company paid Thompson, and most of Jan's lot went directly to Aunt Ethel for household expenses. He had, therefore, no spare dollars to spread around.

The deep, dank silence was marred only by the scraping of silver on china. It was as if they all had secrets which they were fearful of giving away to each other, or as if they could say nothing but things so awful that they wouldn't even let Jan hear them. The old house, with its ship models on the mantel and the great timbers across the ceilings and the hurricane lanterns hung along the walls would have been much louder had it had no occupants at all.

Jan was glad when the gloomy footman put indifferent coffee before them. If he was careful, he could gulp it down and get away without a thing being said to him.

But his luck didn't hold. "Jan," said Nathaniel heavily, "I trust you will be home this evening." The question implied that Jan was never to be found at home, but always in some dive somewhere, roistering.

"Yes," said Jan.

"You saw fit to leave today when I needed your signature. When I finally found you, I had only time to get the most urgent matters attended to. You are too careless of these serious matters. There are at least twenty letters which only you can write, unfortunately. I am forced to demand that you finish them tonight. If I but had your complete power of attorney, you would save me much needless labor. I have so many things to do already that if I were six men with twelve hands I couldn't get them done in time."

Strangely enough, it came as welcome news to Jan. He almost smiled. "I am sorry I can't be of more help, but I'll be glad to do the letters tonight."

Nathaniel grunted as much as to say that Jan better if he knew what was good for him. And Jan took the grunt as a cue for his departure. Swiftly he made his way to his apartments, fearful that this wouldn't come out the way he hoped it would.

The first thing he did was strip off his clothes and

duck under a shower. He came forth in an agony of haste, losing everything and finding it and losing it again as he swiftly assembled himself. His wardrobe was able to offer very little, as Aunt Ethel purchased most of his clothing and did little purchasing. But the dark-blue suit was neatly pressed and his cravat was nicely tied. He had no more than finished slicking back his blond hair when a knock sounded.

Hurriedly he flung himself into his chair by the desk and scooped up a book. Then he called, "Come in," as indifferently as he could.

Alice Hall stepped into the room. As Nathaniel's secretary it was her duty, two or three times a week, to call in the evening to let Jan catch up on company correspondence. She was the last of six stenographers, and ever since she had first taken the job, four months before, Jan had lain awake nights trying to figure out a way to make certain that she would hold her job. It was not so much that she was beautiful—though she was that—and it wasn't entirely because she was the only one who did not seem to look down upon him. Jan had tried in vain to turn up the answer. She was a lady, there was no denying it, and she was far better educated than most stenographers. She did not make him feel at ease at all, but neither did she make him feel uneasy. When he had first beheld her, he had had a hard time breathing.

Her large blue eyes were as impersonal as the turquoise orbs of the idol by the wall. She was interested, it seemed, in nothing but doing her immediate job. Still, there was something about her; something unseen but felt, as the traveler can sense the violence of a slumbering volcano under his feet. Her age was near Jan's own, and she had arrived at that estate without leaving anything unlearned behind her. There was almost something resentful about her; but that, too, was never displayed.

Now she put down her briefcase and took off her small hat and swagger coat and seated herself at a distance from him, placing her materials on a small table before her. She arranged several letters in order and then stepped over to the blackwood desk and laid them before Jan, who, to all signs, was deeply immersed in a treatise on aerodynamics.

Truth told, he was afraid to notice her, not knowing anything to say besides that which had brought her there and not wanting to talk about such matters to her.

She twitched the papers and still he did not look up. Finally she said, "You're holding that book upside down."

"What? Oh . . . oh, yes, of course. These diagrams, you see—"

"Shall we begin on the letters? This one on top is from the Steamship Owners Alliance, asking your attendance at a conference in San Francisco. I have noted the reply on the bottom."

"Oh, yes. Thank you." He looked studiously at the letter, his face very red. "Yes, that's right. I won't be able to attend."

"I didn't think you would," she said unexpectedly.

"Uh?"

"I said I was sure you wouldn't. They asked you, but Mr. Green will go instead."

"He wouldn't want me to go," said Jan. "He . . . knows much more about it than I."

"You're right."

Jan detected, to his intense dismay, something like pity in her voice. Pity or contempt; they were brothers, anyway.

"But he really does," said Jan. "He wouldn't like it if I said I would go."

"He'll be the only nonowner there."

"But he has full authority—"

"Does he?" She was barely interested now. Jan thought she looked disappointed about something. "Shall we get on with these letters?"

"Yes, of course."

For the following two hours he stumbled through the correspondence, taking most of his text from Alice Hall's suggestions. She wrote busily and efficiently and, at last, closed her notebook and put on her hat and coat.

"Do you have to go?" said Jan, surprising himself. "I mean, couldn't I send for some tea and things? It's late."

"I'll be up half the night now, transcribing."

"Oh . . . will you? But don't you finish these at the office in the morning?"

"Along with my regular work? A company can buy a lot for forty dollars a week."

"Forty . . . but I thought our stenographers got sixty!"

"Oh, do you know that much about it?"

"Why . . . yes." He was suddenly brightened by an idea. "If you have to work tonight, perhaps I had better drive you home. It's quite a walk up to the car line–"

"I have my own car outside. It's a fine car when it runs. Good night."

He was still searching for a reply when she closed the door behind her. He got up, suddenly furious with himself. He went over to the fireplace and kicked at the logs, making sparks jump frighteningly up the flue. In the next fifteen minutes he thought of fifteen hundred things to say to her, statements which would swerve her away from believing him a weak mouse, holed up in a cluttered room. And that thought stopped him and sent him into a deep chair to morosely consider the truth of his simile. Time and again he had vowed to tell them all. Time and again something had curled up inside of him to forbid the utterance.

Sunk in morbid reverie, he failed to hear Aunt Ethel enter and indignantly turn out the lights without seeing him in the chair. He failed to see that the fire burned lower and lower until just one log smoldered on the grate. He failed to hear the clock strike two o'clock, and so the night advanced upon him.

With a start he awoke without knowing that he had been asleep. He was cold and aching and aware of something wrong near him. Once again sounded the creepy scratch and Jan stood up, shaking and staring intently into the dark depths of the room. Some one or something was there. He did not want to turn on the light but he knew that he must. He found the lamp beside the chair and pulled its cord. The blinding glare whipped across the room to throw his caller into full relief.

The curtains were blowing inward from the open window, and the papers were stirring on the blackwood desk. And in the corner by the copper jar stood Frobish, nervous with haste, a knife peeling back ribbons of lead from the seal. For an instant, so intent was the interloper, he did not become aware of the light. And then he whirled about, facing Jan.

Frobish's eyes were hot and his face drawn. There was danger in his voice. "I had to do this. I've been half crazy for hours thinking about it. I am going to open this copper jar, and if you try to stop me—" The knife glittered in his fingers.

It was very clear to Jan that he confronted a man whose entire life was concentrated upon one object and who was now driven to a deed which, had conditions been otherwise, would have horrified no one more than Professor Frobish. But, with his goal at hand, it would take more than the strength of one man to stop him.

"You said you promised," said Frobish. "I have nothing to do with that. You are not opening the jar, and you were not commissioned to see that it was never opened by anyone. Your cousin was protecting only you and himself. He cared nothing about anyone else. If any harm comes from this, it is not on your head. Stay where you are and be silent." He again attacked the stopper.

Jan, his surprise leaving him, looked anxiously along the wall. But there were no weapons on this side of the room except an old pistol which was not loaded and, indeed, was too rusty to offer even a threat.

A sudden spasm of outrage shook him. That this fellow should presume to break in here and meddle with what was his was swelled with years of resentment against all the countless invasions of his privacy and the confiscations of his possessions.

Shaking and white, Jan advanced across the room.

Frobish whirled around to face him. "Stand back! I warn you this is no ordinary case. I won't be balked! This research is bigger than either you or I." His voice was mounting toward hysteria.

Jan did not stop. Watchful of the knife, unable to understand how the professor could go to such lengths as using it, he came within a pace of Frobish. Frobish backed up against the wall, breathing hard, swinging the weapon up to the level of his shoulder.

"I've dreamed for years of making such a discovery. You cannot stop me now!"

"Be quiet or people will hear you," said Jan, cooled a little by the sight of the knife. "You can leave now and nothing will have happened."

Frobish was quick to sense the change. He reached out and shoved Jan away from him, to whirl and again to pry at the stopper.

Jan seized hold of his shoulder and whirled him about. "You're insane! This is my house and that jar is mine. You have no right, I tell you."

Savagely Frobish struck at him, and Jan, catching the blow on the point of his chin, dropped to the floor, turned halfway about. Groggily he shook his head and rose, still unwilling to believe that Frobish could fail to listen to reason, unable to understand that he was dealing with forces and desires greater than he could ever hope to control.

Once more Frobish flung him away and would have followed up, but behind him there was a sound

like escaping steam. He forgot Jan and faced the jar instantly to stumble back from it. Jan remained frozen to the floor a dozen feet away.

Black smoke was coiling into the dark shadows of the ceiling, mushrooming slowly outward, rolling into itself with ominous speed. Frobish backed against a chair and stopped, hands flung up before his face, while over him, like a shroud, the acrid vapors began to drop down.

Jan coughed from the fumes and blinked with tears which were stung from his eyes. The stopper was not wholly off the jar and stayed on the edge, teetering until the last of the smoke was past, when it dropped with a dull sound to the floor.

The smoke eddied more swiftly against the beams. It became blacker and blacker, more and more solid, drawing in and in again and finally beginning to pulsate as though it breathed.

Something hard flashed at the top of it and then became two spiked horns, swiftly accompanied by two gleaming eyes the size of meat platters. Two long tusks, polished and sharp, squared the awful cavern of a mouth. Swiftly then the smoke became a body girt with a blazing belt, two arms tipped by clawed fingers, two tree-like legs ending in hoofs, split-toed and as large across as an elephant's foot. The thing was covered with shaggy hair except for the face and the tail which lashed back and forth now in agitation.

The thing knelt and flung up its hands and cried: "There is no God but Allah, the all-merciful and compassionate. Spare me!"

Jan was frozen. The fumes were still heavy about him, but now there penetrated a wild-animal smell which made his man's soul lurch within him in memory of days an æon gone.

Frobish, recovered now, and seeing that the thing was wholly on the defensive, straightened up.

"There is no God but Allah. And Sulayman is the lord of the earth!" cried the Ifrit.

"Get up," said Frobish. "We care less than nothing about Allah, and Sulayman has been dead these many centuries. I have loosed you from your prison and in return there are things I desire."

The Ifrit's luminous, yellow eyes played up and down the puny mortal before him. Slowly an evil twist came upon the giant lips. A laugh rumbled deep in him like summer thunder—a laugh wholly of contempt.

"So, it is as I thought it might be. You are a man, and you have loosed me. And now you speak of a reward." The Ifrit laughed again. "Sulayman, you say, is dead?"

"Naturally. Sulayman was as mortal as I."

"Yes, yes. As mortal as you. Man who freed me, you behold before you Zongri, king of the Ifrits of the Barbossi Isles. For thousands of years have I been in that jar. Would you like to know what I thought about?"

"Well?" said Frobish peevishly.

"Mortal man, the first five hundred years I vowed that the man who set me free would have all the riches in the world. But no man freed me. The next five hundred years I vowed that the man who let me out would have life everlasting, even as I. But no man let me out. I waited then for a long, long time and then, at long last, I fell into a fury at my captivity and I vowed— You are sure you wish to know, mortal man?"

"Yes!"

"Then know that I vowed that the one who set me free would meet with instant death!"

Frobish paled. "You are a fool, as I have heard that all Ifrits are fools. But for me you would have stayed there the rest of eternity. Tonight I had to break into that man's house to loose you. It is he who has held you captive, who would not let you go."

"A vow is never broken. You have freed me and therefore you shall die!" A thunderous scowl settled upon his face and he edged forward on his knees, unable to stand against the fourteen-foot ceiling.

Frobish backed up hastily.

The Ifrit glanced about him. Near at hand were the Malay krisses and upon the largest he fastened, wrenching it from the wall and bringing the rest of the board down with a clatter. The great executioner's blade looked like a toothpick in his fist.

Frobish strove to dash out of the room but the Ifrit raked out with his claws and snatched him back, holding him a foot from the floor.

"A vow," muttered Zongri, "is a vow." And so saying he released Frobish, who again tried to run.

The blade flashed and there was a crunching sound as of a cleaver going through ham. Split from crown to waist, Frobish's corpse dropped to the floor, staining the carpet for a yard about.

Jan winced as something moist splashed against his hand and swiftly he scuttled back. The movement attracted the Ifrit's attention and again the claws raked out and clutched. Jan, assailed by fuming breath and sick with the sight of death, shook like a rag in a hurricane.

The Ifrit regarded him solemnly.

"Let me go," said Jan.

"Why?"

"I did not free you."

"You kept me captive for years. That one said so."

"You cannot," chattered Jan, "kill a man for letting you free and then kill another for . . . for not letting you free."

"Why not?"

"It . . . it is not logical!"

Zongri regarded him for a long time, shaking him now and then to start him shivering anew. Finally he said: "No, that is so. It is not logical. You did not let me free, and I said no vow about you. You are Mohammedan?"

"N-n-no!"

"Hm-m-m." Again Zongri shook him. "You are no friend of Sulayman's?"

"I . . . n-n-no!"

"Then," said the Ifrit, "it would not be right for me to kill you." He dropped him to the floor and looked around. "But," he added, "you held me captive for years. He said you did. That cannot go unpunished."

Jan hugged the moist floor, waiting for doom to blanket him.

"I cannot kill you," said Zongri. "I made no vow. Instead . . . instead, I shall lay upon you a sentence. Yes, that is it. A sentence. You, mortal one, I sentence"—and laughter shook him for a moment—"to eternal wakefulness. And now I am off to Mount Kaaf!"

There was a howling sound as of winds. Jan did not dare open his eyes for several seconds, but when he did he found that the room was empty.

Unsteadily he got to his feet, stepping gingerly around the dead man, and then discovered to his dismay that he himself was now smeared with blood.

The executioner's knife had been dropped across the body and, with some wild thought of trying to bring the man back to life, Jan laid it aside, shaking the already cooling shoulder.

Realizing that that was a fruitless gesture, he again got to his feet. For the first time in his life he did not want to be alone. He wanted lights and people about him. Yes, even Green or Thompson.

He laid his hand upon the door, but before he could pull, it crashed in on his chest—and he found himself staring into a crowd in the hall.

Two prowl-car men, guns in hand, were in front. A servant stood behind them and after that he could see the strained faces of Aunt Ethel and Thompson and Green.

A flood of gladness went through him, but he was too shocked to speak. Mutely he pointed toward Frobish's body and tried to tell them that the Ifrit had gone through the window. But other voices swirled about him.

"Nab him, Mike; it's open and shut," said the sergeant.

Mike nabbed Jan.

"Deader'n a door nail," said Mike, looking at the bisected corpse. "Open and shut." He took out a book and flipped it open. "How long ago did you do it?"

"About five minutes!" said Thompson. "When I first heard the voices in here and sent for you, I didn't expect anything like this to happen. But I heard the sound of the knife and then silence."

"Five minutes, eh?" said the sergeant, wetting the end of his pencil and writing. "And what was this all about, you?"

Jan recovered his voice. "You . . . you think I did this thing?"

"Well?" said Mike. "Didn'tcha?"

"No!" shouted Jan. "You don't understand. That jar—"

"Fell on him, I suppose."

"No, no! That jar—"

Intelligence flashed in Aunt Ethel's needle-point eyes. She flung herself upon Jan, weeping. "Oh, my poor boy. How could you do such an awful thing?"

Jan, startled, tried to shake her off, urgently protesting to the sergeant all the while. "I told him not to, but he broke through the window and pried at the stopper—"

"Who?" said Mike.

"I'll handle this," said the sergeant in reproof.

"He means Professor Frobish, his guest," said Thompson. "The professor came to see him about an Arabian ship model this afternoon."

"Huh, murdered his guest, did he? Mike, you hold on here while I send for the homicide squad."

"Don't!" shouted Jan. "You've got it all wrong. Frobish broke in here to let—"

"Save it for the Judge," said Mike, shaking him to quiet him down.

Jan glared at those around him. Thompson was looking at him in deep sorrow. Aunt Ethel was wiping her eyes with the hem of her dressing gown. And all the while Nathaniel Green was pacing up and down the room, squashing fist into palm and muttering: "A murder. A Palmer a murderer. Oh, how can such things keep happening to me! The publicity—and just when the government was offering a subsidy. I knew it, I knew it. He was always strange, and now see what he's done. I should have watched him more closely. It's my fault, all my fault."

"No, it's mine," wept Aunt Ethel. "I've tried to be a mother to him and he repays us by killing his guest in our house. Oh, think of the papers!"

It went on and on. It went on for the benefit of the newspapermen who came swarming in on the heels of such a name as Palmer. It went on for the benefit of the homicide squad. Over and over until Jan was sick and wobbly.

The fingerprint men were swift in their work. The photographers took various views of the corpse.

And then an ambulance backed up beside the Black Maria, and while Frobish was basketed into the former, Jan, under heavy guard, was herded into the latter.

And as they drove away, the last thing he heard was Aunt Ethel's wail to a late-coming newsman that here was gratitude after all that she had done for him and wasn't it awful, awful, awful? Wasn't it? Wasn't it? Wasn't it?

THREE

Jan was too stunned by the predicament to protest any further; he went so willingly—or nervelessly—wherever he was shoved that the officers concluded there was no more harm left in him for the moment. Besides, a gang of counterfeiters was occupying the best cells and so a little doubling was in order. Jan found himself thrust into a cubicle, past a pale, snake-eyed fellow, and then the door clanged authoritatively and the guard marched away.

Seeing the cell and the cellmate, and believing it was a cell and a cellmate were two entirely different things. Jan sat down on a bunk and looked woodenly straight ahead. He was in that frame of mind where men behold disaster at every side but are so thoroughly drenched with it that they begin to discount it. It was even a somewhat solacing frame of mind. Nothing worse than this could possibly happen. Unlucky fate had opened the bag and pulled out everything at once and so, by lucid reason, it was impossible for said unlucky fate to have any further stock still hidden.

"That's my bunk," snarled the cellmate.

Jan obediently moved to the other berth to discover that it was partly unhinged so that a man had to sleep with his head below his feet. Further, the cellmate had robbed it of blankets to benefit his own couch and so had exposed a questionable mattress.

Jan's deep sigh sucked the smell of disinfectant so

deeply into his lungs that he went into a spasm of coughing.

"Lunger?" said the cellmate indifferently.

"Beg pardon?"

"I said, have y'got it inna pipes?"

"What?"

"Skiput."

"Really," said Jan, "I don't understand you."

"Oh, a swell, huh? What'd they baste you wit'?"

"Er—"

"How's it read? What's the yarn? What'd they book you for?" said the fellow with great impatience. "Murder? Arson? Bigamy—"

"Oh," said Jan with relief. "Oh, yes, certainly." And then the enormity of the error came back to him, and he grew agitated. "I'm supposed to have murdered a man—but I didn't do it!"

"Sure not. Hammer, lead or steel?" Hastily, to clarify himself: "How'd you do it?"

"But I didn't!" said Jan. "It's all a horrible mistake."

"Sure. Was it a big shot?"

"There wasn't any shooting. It was an executioner's sword."

"Exe—Say! You do things with a flair, doncha?"

"But I didn't do it!"

"Well, hell, who said you did? What was the stiff's name?"

"Stiff? Oh . . . Professor Frobish of the university."

"Brain wizard, huh? Never liked 'em myself. How come the slash party in the first place? I mean, how'd it happen?"

"That's what's so terrible about it," said Jan, so deep in misery that he did not fully comprehend what he was saying. "I had a copper jar in my room and Frobish insisted upon opening it, and when I refused him he returned in the night and pried the stopper out of it because he knew it might contain an Ifrit." Mistaking the popeyes for sympathy, Jan went on: "And it *did* contain an Ifrit that Sulayman had bottled up, and when the thing came out it took down a sword and killed Frobish, and when the police got there they didn't give me a chance to explain. They thought I did it, and so here I am!"

"What," said the cellmate, "is an Ifrit? Do you eat it or spend it?"

"An Ifrit? Oh. Why, an Ifrit is a demon of the tribes of the jinn. Some people call them jinnis or geniis. They seem to have vanished from the earth, although there is evidence that they were once very numerous."

"What . . . what do they look like?"

"Why, they're about fifteen feet tall, and they've got horns and a spiked tail—"

"A sniffer."

"What?"

"I said I didn't think you looked like a sniffer when I first seen you."

"I don't understand."

"Sure. Well, go on, don't let me stop you," he said indulgently. "Fifteen feet tall with horns and a spiked tail—"

Jan frowned. "You don't believe me."

"Sure, I believe you. Hell, who wouldn't believe you? Why, I seen worse than that before I finally yanked myself up on the wagon. Once I lamped a whole string of such things. They was hangin' to each other's tails with one hand and carrying purple sedans in the other. And—"

"You doubt my word?"

"Hell, no, buddy. Just sit down and be calm. No use frettin' about a little thing like that, see? Sure. I know all about these there—what did you say you called 'em?"

"Ifrits!"

"Sure, that's right. You've been done dirt, that's

sure. But all you gotta do is tell the truth to the judge and he'll do the rest."

"You think I've got a chance?"

"Listen, pal, I'm in here for shaking down a gent for eight hundred bucks. That's what they say I did. I didn't, of course. But if I think I've got a story lined up—geez, you must be a genius."

The other's volunteered information brought Jan slightly out of himself, enough to realize that his cell-mate was also answering to the law. With this in common, Jan took interest in him.

"They arrested you, too?"

"Hell, no, buddy, I use this for a hotel. Look, I don't know where they dug you up or who you are—"

"My name is Jan Palmer."

"O.K., your name is Jan Palmer. Fine. But would you please tell me how a gent can live all his life in these United States without finding out a thing or two? Palmer, I hate to say it, but unless you smarten up you ain't got an onion's chance in Spain. Me, I know the ropes. There ain't nobody in the racket that knows more about what's what than Diver Mullins. Now listen to me. You give this cockeyed yarn of yours the bounce and think of somethin' logical. Otherwise, my innercent pal, they'll swing you by the neck until you're most awful dead."

Jan was jolted. He peered nearsightedly at his cell-mate, seeing him truly for the first time. There was no mistaking the evil in that face. It was narrow as a ferret's and of an unhealthy pallor. The eyes flicked up and down and around and about in incessant sentinel duty. Shabby and wasted though he was, there was still a certain vitality in the fellow.

"But . . . but," said Jan, "I told you the truth. An Ifrit came out of the jar—"

"Look, pal," said Diver Mullins, "I ain't doubtin' your word. I believe every syllable. But I ain't the judge, and when you spin that cockeyed story before a jury they'll laugh at you. Now, take me. I ain't in here for the first time. No, sir! I know my business. I was located in possession of eight hundred smacks that a sap lost. That's an insult. If I'd have taken it offn him in a crowd, do you suppose he ever would have knowed about it?"

"You mean you had another fellow's money," decoded Jan.

"Go to the head of the class. Now another gent would say he found it on the sidewalk or some place and get himself laughed at. But not me. Another fellow would say he didn't know how it got in his pocket. But not me! Them dodges has mildew on 'em. Now, I figger—"

But Jan had relapsed into his own woes and scarcely heard Diver Mullins' plot to put the entire blame upon another pickpocket and place himself in a savior light. Jan, accountably weary, lay back on the tipsy bunk and gave himself over to dreary speculation.

He retraced the activities of the night and found them to be anything but reassuring. And, to escape from their damning possibilities, he dwelt upon the inconsequentialities. He was, for instance, almost certain that Zongri had spoken in Arabic. He, Jan, spoke no Arabic so far as he knew. Of course, Frobish would understand the language, but how could it be that Jan had come into the sudden possession of such knowledge? Perhaps it wasn't really Arabic. Jan didn't know enough to be certain on that score, just as he was too hazy to analyze the Ifrit's "eternal wakefulness."

The puzzle was far too much for him and his tired, event-shocked brain gave it up. In a few moments he was falling steeply into exhausted slumber.

The thing which happened immediately thereafter was the turning point in the life of Jan Palmer for one—even beyond the effect of the murder.

FOUR

He went to sleep, but he didn't go to sleep. He had a sensation of dropping straight down. Heretofore he had been aware, in common with all men, of a delicious period of semiwakefulness preceding and succeeding slumber. But from that period he had always gone into a deep sleep—so far as he knew—or had come fully awake. Now he felt as though the world had been obscured by a veil which no more than dropped than it was ripped startlingly aside.

A hail rang hysterically in his ears: "Breakers two points off the sta'b'd b-o-o-o-o-w! *B-r-r-reakers* two points off the sta'b'd bow! Captain, for the love of God, we're on the rocks!"

Jan had scarcely lifted his hand and felt the spokes of a helm under his fingers when he was jarred fully awake and almost into sleep again by a most tremendous blow which rocketed him all the way across the quarterdeck, from binnacle to scupper. He brought up against the rail and lifted himself cautiously.

The quiet vessel was suddenly bedlam. The captain's roars seconding the still-braying lookout, the crew spilled helter-skelter from the fo'c's'le, rubbing their eyes, scarcely knowing what they were doing, but automatically taking their stations.

The masts swooped back and forth across the stars as the captain's savage hands spun the helm. The thunder of breakers could be plainly heard now and, lifting himself a little more, Jan beheld their phosphorescent line which swiftly swung parallel to the ship.

"Let go the port sheets!" bellowed the captain. "Take in on the sta'b'd main sheet!"

Canvas cannonaded in the fresh wind and then the deck leaped under them as the billowing white cliff tautened in the gloom. On a close port tack the big vessel picked up a bone and scudded back into the safety of the sea.

"Make fast!" roared the captain.

"Lively now," cried a mate somewhere in the waist.

The ship surged ahead anew as the sails were more precisely trimmed and then, one by one, the crew made their ways back to the fo'c's'le and more sleep.

When all was in order, the captain turned the wheel over to another man and gave him a course and then, with both hands on his hips, he planted his feet solidly on the deck and glared about him.

"Now! Where's that helmsman?"

Jan shivered, and he had every right. The captain loomed into the stars, and the gleam of the binnacle which fell upon his face displayed two glittering fangs. From the flame of his eye and the posture Jan knew that once again, in less than four hours, he had run afoul of an Ifrit.

He had no slightest inkling of what he was doing there or why, and he had no time to consider it.

Shaking, he came upright, holding hard to the rail.

"So you're still here," said the captain, advancing. Suddenly his hand shot out and he gripped Jan by the shirt front and shook him clear of the deck, slamming him back to the planking.

"Asleep! Asleep at the wheel! Why, you ugly pup, I ought to knock every tooth out of your ugly face! I ought to smash your skull like an egg! Do you realize what you did? Has it leaked through your thick skull that you put us miles and miles off our course and almost killed us to a man on the Faybran shoals? Sleep, will you—" And again he lifted Jan up and threw him down. With the biggest boot Jan had ever

arrived there. That he had no recollection whatever of arriving had him half convinced that he wasn't there at all.

He saw a mirror across the room from him and, with sudden suspicion, approached it. He was jolted so that he took two steps backward. He recovered himself and peered more closely at his image.

Yes, now that he made a closer examination, it was himself. But what a difference there was! He, Jan Palmer, was a thin-faced, anæmic fellow, but this brute who was staring back at him was bold of visage, brawny of arm, tall and—yes, he had to admit it—not bad at all to look upon. But the knife scar which ran from the lobe of his ear diagonally to his jawbone—where had that come from? He felt of it and peered more closely at it. He didn't really object to it at all because it didn't mar his looks but, in truth, rather gave him an air.

Puzzled, he looked down at himself. His blue pants incased very muscular and shapely legs. His bare chest was matted with blond hair. He looked back at his image as though it might solve the riddle for him.

"Tiger!" cried a voice in the passageway.

Jan started and saw that the captain was just then entering. The captain looked shocked.

"In here? Well, of all the gall! By God, I do believe there's something gone wrong with you. Don't you know enough to wait outside? Come here!"

Jan obeyed. Roughly the captain forced him down [illegible] and inspected his skull with great perplex- [illegible] chance to realize that this Ifrit was, [illegible] than Zongri. Either that [illegible] than he had [illegible]

The captain once again removed his cap and scratched one of his pointed ears. "And scared, too. I never thought I'd live to see that. Tiger, scared. By God, if this is a game, you won't enjoy it."

"It's no trick," said Jan. "I don't know anything about it."

"Hm-m-m. It's just barely possible— See here, give me the straight of this and no lying! What are you up to?"

Jan spread his hands hopelessly. "I'm not up to anything! One minute I am sleeping in a jail and the next I am leaning on the helm of this ship. How I can tell you when I don't know myself—"

"Jail? For God's sake, where?"

"Why, in Seattle, of course."

"Where?"

"Seattle, Washington."

"That's one port I never heard of, anyway. Go ahead and talk, Tiger, and make it good. I know you've seen plenty of jails, but that particular one has escaped me. Go on. What did you do to get in jail?"

"I didn't do anything! They thought I'd killed a Professor Frobish that came to see me but I didn't do it. He wanted to open a copper jar and I wouldn't let him, so he came back at night and did it anyway. I was asleep in a chair but I woke up too [illegible] him. And when the Ifrit came out—"

"Copper jar? Ifrit? Go on!"

"I'm not!"

"But Zongri was captured and entombed by Sulayman thousands of years ago! I remember hearing about it. He was king of the Barbossi Isles and he refused to change faith with the others." Suddenly he grew very agitated and stalked about the room. Abruptly he again confronted Jan. "See here, did this Zongri say anything to you? Did he do anything?"

"Yes. He said he was going to sentence me to eternal wakefulness—"

"Hush!" said the captain, going swiftly to the port and slamming it shut. He closed the door and then came back to the bed with the air of a conspirator. "Zongri said that?"

"Yes. And then I was arrested and taken to jail because they thought—"

"To Shatan with that! Oh, the fool, the fool! Eternal wakefulness!" The captain slammed a fist into his palm with the wish that Zongri was in between. "It's like him. He almost runs my ship on the rocks! He was at the bottom of the war with Sulayman and all our woes since. And now—" He eyed Jan. "Tiger, if you are telling me lies—"

"It's true! I swear it's true."

"Hm-m-m. Perhaps. If it weren't for the ch
you. I wouldn't credit any of it. But you
well. . . . Hm-m-m. You swear to this, you sa

"Certainly."

"All right. So be it. Mr. Malek!"

The mate clattered down the ladder and thr
head in the door.

"Mr. Malek, you will take Tiger down to the
and post a reliable Muid over him. Understand t
Tiger is not to talk to anyone, you hear? Absolutely
one! When we get into port we'll find out what to d
with him."

Malek took hold of Jan's collar and jerked him to his feet.

"Count on me," said Malek. "He won't see a soul."

"Your head will answer for it if he does."

"That's all right with me," said Malek, jerking Jan down the passageway and into the bowels of the ship.

FIVE

Jan went round and round his small cell like a white rat spinning about a pole. And his head went faster than he. He shook the bars and yelled at the departing mate, but Malek had no further heed for him. Growing terror caused him to shout at the guard, but the Marid, too, was most indifferent. And so it was that Jan dizzied himself by pacing the walls. He could stand a berating, perhaps, and even face a flogging without really cracking, but this situation was of the stuff of which madness was made. He had long ceased to doubt that he was here, because, after all, he *was* here. And what in the name of God did they mean to do with him?

Again he besought information from the Marid. The guard was small, with a solitary eye in the middle of his head and a twist to his back, garbed in a single cloak. His lack of shoes was backed by ample reason. He had hooves.

"Be quiet," said the Marid at last. "Better you sleep." And with that he faced the other way and was wholly deaf.

At long, long last Jan wearied himself to exhaustion. He sank down on the pile of blankets and buried his face in his arms, striving to gather and tie the loose ends of his nerves.

His strange position was bad enough, but not even to be himself! Who and what was this Tiger? True, he had some slight resemblance to Jan Palmer, but that was not enough. Tiger was known here, known for a bad character, it seemed. *But* if Jan Palmer was now Tiger, where was Tiger?

He could not answer that and the weight of it was the proverbial straw. His mind went wholly blank and he lay in apathy. Once or twice he reasoned that this was still the jail. But each time he lifted his head to prove it, there was the Marid in all his evil dignity. Yes, and in the damp air was the hissing sound of the clean hull carving through the waves, that and the sing of wind through rigging, far, far above.

This was a sea, an unknown sea. This was the brig of a ship, the like of which had not sailed the seas for a hundred years and more.

It was too much. And at last Jan dozed, drifting more deeply into slumber.

To no avail.

He had no more than shut his eyes when he was startled by the slam of iron-barred doors and the rattle of dishes which immediately followed. Voices were hollow in the concrete hall and Jan sat up. He looked carefully all around him.

But it was no Marid at the door, but a blue-coated policeman engaged in shoving a tray of food under the door.

"You gonna sleep forever?" said Diver Mullins, scraping half-heartedly at his lathered face. "Y'rolled and tossed all night long. I hardly got a chance to close m'eyes."

"I . . . I'm sorry," said Jan, blinking at the cell around him and experiencing an uplift of heart. Thankfully he took a deep breath, only to choke on the disinfectant in the air. But that hardly lessened his thankfulness.

It was quite plain to him now that the ship and the Ifrits had been of the substance of nightmares. And, more than that, when he looked in the glass and found that Jan Palmer's sickly visage gazed back at him, he wanted to shout for joy.

"Geez, for a gent that's about to be stretched," said

Diver Mullins, "you sure can put on the happy act."

"Beg pardon?" said Jan.

"It ain't right," said Diver petulantly. "You commit a moider after supper and you wake up singin' like a canary bird."

"Murder?"

"Don't tell me," said Diver, "that you went and forgot about it."

Jan groaned and sank back on his bunk. He held his face in his hands to steady himself as the black ink of memory drowned him. Murder. He was in here for murder. An Ifrit named Zongri had killed a man named Frobish and now they were going to hang a hopelessly innocent Palmer for the deed.

"Now I done it," said Diver. "I'd ruther you'd chirp than beller, my fine-fettered friend. Cheer up. They only hang a man once." So saying he hauled the tray close to him and speared the soggy hotcakes with every evidence of appetite. "C'mon and eat."

Jan, mechanically ready to obey almost anybody, accordingly hitched a stool up to the table and took the offered plate. He even went so far as to butter the dough blankets and convey a forkful to his mouth. And then he found out what he was doing and gagged. He crawled to his bed and sprawled upon it, face down.

"They ain't as bad as that," said Diver. "Course, in lotsa jails they serve lots better belly paddin', but my motto is to take what y'can get your hooks into and don't ask too many questions. Nobody never measured me for a noose or even said they was going to, so I ain't had a lot of experience. But, hell, you hadn't ought to let it get you down like that. You get borned and then you live awhile and then somebody knocks you off or you get pneumonia or something and there you are. Now, take me, I don't have the faintest notion of how I'll meet m' Maker. The information ain't to be had. But you, now, that's different. It's all cut and dried and you ain't got to worry about it any more. So that's that. C'mon and have some hotcakes before they get cold."

As Jan made no move to answer the invitation, Diver philosophically conveyed the second portion to his own plate and, with the usual appetite of the very thin, put them easily down and finally, having cleared the tray, looked mournfully under the napkins to locate more. His search unavailing, he slid it back into the corridor and fell into a conversation with a counterfeiter across the block. With great leisure, as men do when they know they have lots of time to pass, they discussed the latest inmate with great thoroughness, and Diver, after fishing for coaxing, finally laid aside an air of mystery and divulged Jan's story.

"Hophead, huh?" said the counterfeiter.

"Yeah, guess so. He don't eat nothin' and that's another reason. He evidently is feelin' the mornin' after, no doubt."

"I know where I can get him some," said the counterfeiter confidentially.

"Yeah? When he gets over his fit, I'll ask him if he wants it. He had nightmares last night fit to shake the place down."

"Yeah, I heard him."

"Snow's pretty awful stuff."

"Ain't it!" said the counterfeiter. "Why, once I had a sniffer in my outfit—Goo-goo, the boys called'm—and this here Goo-goo—"

Jan tried not to listen, even stuffing his ears with the edge of the blanket, but one story led to another and finally they got on the subject of being hanged.

"So they sprung the trap three times on this gent," said the counterfeiter, "and it wouldn't sag with him. They'd take him off and put him back and try her again and still she wouldn't work. Well, the guy fainted finally, but they brought him around and put him on the trap once more. Well, sir, this time she sure worked. He dropped like a rock and the rope snapped his spine like you'd crack walnuts. Three times and it don't work."

"Leave it to the law," said Diver. "They can't even hang a man straight."

"Somebody coming," said the counterfeiter.

The block fell silent, watching the approach of the visitors. All but Jan clung to the bars, for he was in a state of coma induced by the late conversations.

"Hiyah, babe," said a jailbird down the row.

"Gee, some looker," said Diver, now that he could see the party.

A series of such comments and calls ran the length of the place and then the party stopped before Jan's door while a jailer, with much important key rattling, got the lock open.

Diver backed up and gave the prostrate Jan a wicked kick to wake him. Resentfully, Jan sat up, about to protest, but all such thought left him when he found that Alice Hall stood before him.

She had carried herself like a sentry through the block just as though the jailbirds did not exist, and now, with a tinge of pity upon her lovely face, she stood taking off her gloves and studying Jan, just as though she were about to begin an operation to change his luck.

"Well, well, well, my boy," said a very, very hearty voice—one which the owner fondly thought capable of carrying him, some day, to the Senate. "What are they doing to you?"

Jan dragged his eyes away from Alice and woke up to the presence of two others in his cell—Shannon, the Bering Steamship's legal-department head, and Nathaniel Green. Shannon was very plump and so fitted his manner to the recognized one for all plump men. He was very hearty, very well met and very reassuring, though there were those—who had, no doubt, lost cases to him—who said it was all sham. The fellow's mouth, in its absence of a sufficient chin and nose, looked like nothing if not a shark's. One supposed he had to turn over on his back to eat, so tightly and immobilely did his fat neck sit in his collar.

Jan looked nervous and was not at all sure that he wanted to talk to these two gentlemen. He resented their presence all the more because Alice Hall was there. He wanted to have her sit on the small stool and hear his flood of grief and then give him very sound advice in return. Didn't her brave face have a tinge of pity in it?

"Have you out in no time," said Shannon, sitting down on Diver's bunk so that Diver had to hastily get out of his way.

"Don't mind me," said Diver resentfully.

Shannon twirled his hat and paid no attention to anything save the crown of the bowler. He was getting serious now, evidently opening up a whole weighty library of immense legal tomes in his head. "Yes, my boy, serious as this is, we should have no difficulty in getting you freed, eh, Mr. Green?"

"Of course," said Green swiftly. He hadn't seated himself at all, and looked as though he was about to hurry off on some important errand or other. "Must be done. The company, you understand, is in no such position that it can bear this publicity. Look," and he jerked a sheaf of papers out of his pocket and tossed them to the bunk beside Jan, where they fanned out into blazing headlines, "Millionaire Ship-owner Slays Professor" and the like.

Jan shuddered when he saw them and drew back.

"Ha-ha, I don't blame you," said Shannon. "But people forget. Never mind that sort of thing. The point is, we want your version of this . . . er . . . crime. Then, we'll demand a bail to be set and take you home." He got serious once more. "Now, to begin, just how did this thing happen?"

It was Alice Hall's cue. She sat down at the rickety table and spread her notebooks to take down the discourse. Jan looked hopelessly at her, hating to have her take his words so cold-bloodedly.

"We haven't much time," said Nathaniel impatiently, glancing at his watch.

"I . . . I don't know how to begin," said Jan.

"Why, at the beginning, of course," said Shannon. "Nothing simpler. When was the first time that you saw this Frobish fellow?"

Jan told them and then, with much prompting, managed to get the story out in its entirety. Very wisely he refrained from following it up with the events of the night just passed. And all the while he spoke, Alice Hall inscribed his words as emotionlessly as though she listened to a dictaphone record. Not so the other two. With increasing frequency Shannon glanced knowingly at Green and Green stared impatiently at Jan as though about to accuse him of lying.

Then, when Jan was through, Shannon's tone was very different from his first. Shannon patted Jan on the knee consolingly as one will a sick animal or perhaps an angry child. "There, there, my boy, we'll do what we can. But . . . er . . . don't you think you might . . . ah . . . modify these statements somewhat? After all, if I wish to have bail set for you, I have to have something I can tell the judge. It's not that we don't believe you . . . but . . . well, courts are strange things and you'll have to trust to my advice and experience in the matter. I shall enter a plea at my discretion. Perhaps," he added to Nathaniel, "I can think of something logical."

Green glanced at his watch. "I've got to be getting back to the office. I've a million things to do before noon."

"Could I speak with you a moment?" said Shannon.

Green irritably acquiesced and they stepped out into the hall where they spoke in low whispers, looking toward the cell now and then. Alice Hall kept her eyes on her notes.

"They don't believe me," said Jan.

The girl looked searchingly at him. "You wonder about it?"

"Why . . . but what happened, happened. I wouldn't lie!"

The shadow of a smile went across her features. "Of course not."

"But it *did* happen that way!" wailed Jan. "And I'll tell you something else. Last night—" But there he stopped and nothing could persuade him to finish.

"You shouldn't keep any of it back," said Alice. "Those gentlemen, presumably, mean to get you out of here, and if you know anything else you should tell them."

"I don't know anything else."

She shrugged. "All right, have it your own way."

"Don't be angry."

"I'm not. Why should I be?"

"But you were."

"Maybe I was. What of it?"

"But why should you be angry?"

"No reason at all," she said with sudden bitterness. "You have a story and you'll stick to it. If you're going to act that way I can tell you truthfully, though it's none of my business, that you'll hang. I don't know—and I don't care, I'm sure!—whether you committed this murder or not. But I do know that you'll have to get yourself out of it the best you can."

"What do you mean?"

"I suppose Green hasn't been waiting—" She suddenly cooled her heat and gave her attention to her notes.

"You mean you think they won't help me?"

"I have nothing to say."

"But you were saying something," pleaded Jan. "If you know anything that might help me—"

"Help you! Nobody can help you! Nobody will ever be able to solve your problems but yourself. I've worked with your company long enough to know that you know nothing about it and care less. You keep yourself locked up in your room, scared to death by an aunt, a secretary and the head of your father's firm. You let Nathaniel Green do what he pleases with accounts—but why am I talking this way? It can do you no good now. I should have spoken months ago. Maybe I was hoping you'd wake up by yourself and find out that you were a man instead of an infant. But you haven't, and now, unless a miracle happens, you'll never have the chance. There! I've said it."

Jan was stunned and scarcely heard Green and Shannon come back until Shannon cleared his throat noisily.

"My boy," said Shannon, "Green and I have talked this thing over. It is quite apparent that you mean to stick to your story."

"It's the truth!"

"Of course it's the truth!" cried Shannon. "But the law is a strange thing. Now, my advice is for you to plead self-defense."

"That would be lying," said Jan.

"Yes, perhaps," said Shannon. And then he gave Green a look which plainly said that he had done what he could. "Very well, young fellow, I shall tell the court your story and ask that you be released on bail. Is that according to your wishes?"

"Certainly!" said Jan.

Green almost smiled but checked himself in time. He glanced at his watch. "I must be getting back. Come along, Miss Hall. Jan, if anything can be done, Mr. Shannon will do it. Don't despair. We're with you to the end."

So saying, Green walked out, followed by the lawyer and Alice Hall, and the door was locked once more.

Diver came out of the corner and looked at the departing backs and then at Jan. "Geez, fellah, how do you do it?"

"Do what?" said Jan dully.

"The dame," said Diver. "Boy, is she a looker! How do you do it, huh?"

"I don't know what you're talking about."

"Oh, boy, are you a deep one! Why, man, if I had a gal like that in love with me—"

"She's not in love with me!"

"No?" and then Diver laughed. "No, sure not. Innocent, that's you. No, sure she ain't in love with you. Why, she was near cryin' when she came in that door, and she almost bawled while she was writin' at the table there and you was spielin' that awful lie of yours."

"She despises me, I know she does."

"Sure. Sure she does, or she thinks she does. But all you'd have to do, feller, is to square up your spine and act like a man and she'd fall in your lap. I'm telling you."

"I'm sure," said Jan with abrupt heat, "that I'm not interested in what you think of Miss Hall!"

Diver was taken aback, more with surprise than anything else. But presently he began to chuckle. "What a pack of wolves," he said.

"Who?"

"Why, that short feller and that lawyer."

"I don't know what you mean."

"If you don't you're blind as a bat, buddy. Friends of yours?"

"Mr. Green is the head of my—that is, the Bering Steamship Corporation."

"Oh boy, I know why those longshoremen go on strike now! Pal, you got three strikes on you and don't know it."

"I fail—"

"You're fanned, feller, fanned. How come you ever got yourself into such a spot seein' the way that Green wants to do you in?"

"I am sure—"

"So am I. I watched him lickin' his chops all the time he was here. What'd you ever do to him?"

"He was my father's best friend."

"And your dearest enemy," said Diver. "Oh, well, what's done is done. But I sure wish I'd had your chance."

"*My* chance!"

"The gal," said Diver with a deep sigh, lying back on his bunk. "Man, I'd almost enjoy bein' accused of murder if I had her feelin' that way about me." And he closed his eyes so langorously that Jan, contrary to all his regular emotions, wanted very badly to kick the guts out of him.

Lunch came and Jan ate a few mouthfuls without any relish. Dinner time found Diver at the tail end of a long discussion with the counterfeiter over the looks of Alice Hall.

At about seven the cell block was brought to the bars again by an opening door. Ignoring all of them, Alice marched down the concrete to Jan's cell but the jailer did not offer to open the door for her.

Jan stood up, blinking and suddenly tongue-tied.

She was very cool and efficient. "Mr. Green asked me to stop by on my way home and tell you that Shannon was unable to have bail set for you."

"You mean," said the jolted Jan, "that I've got to stay here?"

Slowly she nodded and then found sudden interest in a package she had under her arm. She thrust it through the bars. "It's all right," she told the officer. "They inspected it at the desk. Your Aunt Ethel . . . er . . . sent this to you."

Jan took it mechanically, trying to think of something to say which might detain her a moment. But he thought of nothing and they stood in an awkward silence for a moment.

"I hope you aren't too uncomfortable," she said at last.

"I . . . I'm all right."

"Well . . . I had better be going."

"Th-thank you for the package from Aunt Ethel and th-thank you for coming."

SIX

Jan Palmer was afraid to open his eyes. When Diver had said that he had rolled and tossed the whole night through, he had been perfectly willing to believe that it had all been a nightmare brought about by his excessive mental perturbation. But right now it didn't at all appear that he was rolling and tossing upon the sagging bunk in the jail. In fact it was quite plain that he was lying on blankets and that he had no bunk but floor under him.

Cautiously he pried open one eyelid and found that he looked through a grilled window upon the back of a Marid. It was not the same Marid at all, but another one who was much uglier—if such could be possible—than the first. This fellow had a ferocious cast to his single eye. He was girt about with a sword which must have weighed thirty pounds, and he leaned upon a pike pole so sharp that it tapered to nothingness rather than to a point.

"Now I'm in for it," moaned Jan.

And he startled himself.

"Now I'll get the galleys."

He blinked and said it over again. "Now I'll get the galleys."

Well, what galleys? And how did he know that there would be any galleys in the neighborhood? Further, what reason did he have to think that galleys would be in use?

But, just the same he was convinced and he sat up,

already experiencing an ache in his back and sinewy arms.

"This is a hell of a note," he uttered. "I'm damned if I'll take it, so help me. Let'm flog me. Let'm string me up by the thumbs. But I'll see 'em all in hell before I'll haul an oar."

Plainly, he thought, such a speech showed that he was delirious. But no, his head wasn't hot.

He stood up. "Hey, you one-eyed farmer, where are we?" Certainly, he shouldn't take such a tone with this vicious-looking Marid. He frightened himself.

The Marid's hoofs knocked sharply as he came around and playfully poked the pike straight at Jan's eyes. Jan dodged back from the grille.

"So, what I hear is a lie," said the Marid. "You plenty smart, you Tiger. Lie, lie, lie. All the time lie. You get yours this time."

"I . . . I haven't lied about anything," said Jan.

"We hear. Nobody talks but we hear just the same. Last night you put us on beach, or almost, which is as bad. You take too much rum, I think. This time you get the galleys, I think. Now sit down before I shove this through your guts. They come for you quick enough."

Jan very tamely seated himself and the pike was withdrawn from the grille. Twice in the next half an hour sailors came by and were fain to linger about the grille, but the Marid poked them on their way.

"I do you a favor," said the Marid after a while. "Them men want to cut you up very bad. If you wasn't too drunk last night, I think, you would not have ever tried to put us up on that shoal."

"I wasn't drunk," said Jan.

"Tiger not drunk! I think that's a good one. I tell that one. You know what shoal that was?"

"No."

"See, you drunk. Everybody know that shoal. The Isle of Fire just behind those shoals and you say you not know! Haw!"

"The Isle of Fire? Never heard of it."

"Oh, no, you never heard of it. You never stood off and on in the ship here listening to Admiral Tyronin's flagship people burn up every one. You never on boat that go in to pull off what men left. Haw! You fool, Tiger. Me, I was with you and you still got burns on your leg. Lie to me, I think, and I take pike to you."

Jan thoughtfully lifted up his wide-bottomed pants and stared at his brawny leg. He was startled both by the strength which was obviously in it and by the white burn marks which were there. Then, too, there was a purple scar which ran from knee to ankle and which plainly bespoke a broadax. He examined it carefully as though it might vanish under his touch and the Marid, glancing through the grille, laughed at what he thought was a joke in pantomime.

"Tiger's memory come back fast enough in galleys," said the Marid. "Good you leave or the crew–"

He was interrupted by the clang of a door which opened and closed, admitting a party of men. They came briskly up to the brig and stopped, grounding their muskets with a large gesture. The captain opened the door of the brig and Jan came carefully out to be thrust instantly between two files of the most evil-looking Marids imaginable.

They faced smartly about, their cloaks swirling, shouldered their arms and marched Jan up a ladder to the deck. The captain made a motion toward the port gangway and the file halted there, tightly ringing Jan.

At some distance a knot of seamen stood, growling among themselves and looking toward the prisoner. But the Marids stood very complacently, hairy hands wrapped about their gun barrels.

Jan blinked in the blazing sunlight which glanced hurtfully back from polished bits and scoured deck and from the wide harbor. Wonderingly he looked about at the ship itself to find that it was not unlike a cromster of the Middle Ages though considerably larger. The sterncastle deck, however, was cut into by the after house and the helm was a large wheel. A conglomerate rig it was, with a lateen on the mizzen, fore and aft on the main, the peaks held up with sprits, with a large square topsail and a t'gl'nt above that and with three huge staysails forward. A sprits'l was furled under the bowsprit, and long abandoned had such "water sails" been in modern usage. A dozen brass cannon, glittering and ferocious, thrust their snouts out from the quarter-deck rail. Two bowchasers loomed on the fo'c'sle head. And all along each side, evidently manned from the deck below, were the muzzles of thirty demi-cannon. Aloft there floated from the now naked peak the strangest flag Jan had ever seen. It was a brilliant scarlet and upon it was emblazoned in gold a wheeling bird of prey. Other streamers there were in plenty but he could not make them out, so bright was the greenish sky.

In the harbor about them lay hundreds of other vessels, both large and small, ranging in style from a Greek corbita to a seventy-four. Small shore-boats, not unlike sampans, scudded back and forth on a brisk breeze, carrying all sorts of passengers. Among these, by far, Ifrits predominated, and it was strange indeed to see peaked caps between their pointed ears and massive rings upon their claw-tipped fingers. It was as though the animal kingdom had blended with the human race and that these men-beasts were mocking the ancient history of their human ancestors.

Such, however, could not be the case as Jan well knew. Ifrits were Ifrits. And if the jinn wished to conquer the sea with ships for war and cargo, eschewing other means of transportation—as far as he could see at the moment—then it was certainly being done.

But about the deck of the vessel on which he stood Jan saw far more human beings than he did Ifrits. In fact only the captain and the mate were of the jinn. The guard about him was made up of ugly little Marids and there were two or three one-eyed demons astroll. But the sailors who worked aloft to put harbor furls on the restive canvas were all human beings, seemingly not much different from any other men Jan had ever seen beyond their devil-may-care aspect.

"I suppose," muttered Jan to himself, staring intently across the blinding way at a long, gilded vessel, obviously a galley, "that I'll get the *Pinchoti*, damn her. She's the worst puller of the lot." And again he startled himself by finding that he knew the names of most of these vessels and, indeed, the names of most of the men about the deck. How he came to know them he was not at all sure.

A werewolf, in his human identity, must often feel the beast stirring uneasily within him, threatening to spring forth uncalled. More and more, as time went along, did Jan experience just that sensation, except that, in his case, it was more like that Malay demon, the weretiger. Scholar that he was, he knew considerable about lycanthropy, but never in his life had he thought to experience such a thing, even in a reasonable way, but now, certainly, things were happening to him which he could not begin to discount. Weretiger was certainly the only name for it. He was vaguely conscious of latent wells of knowledge within him, of information which he could almost—but not quite—bring to the surface of his brain. It was as though he had always known these things but was suffering, at the moment, a slight lapse of memory.

He gazed critically at the work of a man working on the huge lateen sail, whom he knew as Lacy. Lacy was bungling the job as usual and it crossed Jan's mind that he bet they needed Tiger's help about the ship just then. Still, he had not the least idea of what he should have been doing.

Further, he found himself in the grip of a very alien impulse. Now nobody in all his life on Earth had ever dreamed that there was an ounce of facetiousness in one Jan Palmer. All jokes he had received with funeral mien, startled when others laughed at them. He had always read of pranks with wondering, puzzled that anyone could get pleasure of out of such things. It must be confessed that Jan Palmer had missed much in the way of education due to the thorough isolation of his youth. Never had he felt the slightest desire to commit, much less understand, what might be called a practical joke.

It was with horror, then, that he found himself contemplating the most foolhardy adventure imaginable. Here he was, packed tight by ten well-armed and doubtlessly zealous Marids, all of them wholly humorless. Here he was charged with God knew what crime and faced with the devil knew what sentence. And the Tiger in him stirred and laughed silently to see that one of the Marids was carrying his musket on his shoulder, hand well away from the trigger which was, providentially or otherwise, within six inches of Jan's face. And the barrel of that musket was pointed up in the general direction of the cantankerous Lacy balanced precariously upon the whippy lateen yard.

"Marvelous," chortled Tiger.

"No! My God, no!" gasped the appalled Jan.

There was the trigger and there was Lacy. The shot would go several feet below the seaman, certainly, but it would crack when it passed through the sail.

"Wonderful!" yearned the laughing Tiger.

Jan covered his face with his hands so that he couldn't see the trigger or Lacy. In a moment the Marid would move temptation far away from Tiger. In a moment Lacy would finish his clumsy furl and come scampering thankfully down from the dizzy heights. In a moment all would be well and Jan would have triumphed.

But the joke was too good. Nobody liked Lacy and Lacy was an avowed coward. Jan's finger slipped and his eye fell upon the burnished trigger. It was too much for him.

Out went his finger quick as a blink. The trigger came back softly. Back came Jan's hand to his innocent side. The match fell, the pan flared, the musket

hands either. This is a case for the crown. Yes, indeed, the crown. Hail my boat," he added to Malek.

Malek shouted to a barge which had been drifting under the quarter and now it was pulled forward to the gangway. It was crammed from gunwale to gunwale with armed men, but they were port sailors and rather given to fat and softness.

"Down with you," said Boli, punching Jan in the back with his sword scabbard as though appalled at the thought of touching him with hand and so soiling it.

Jan started down the ladder. Along the rail stood the ship's fickle company, wholly won again by the incident of Lacy.

"S'long, Tiger."

"Give'm hell, Tiger."

"Give her majesty m'love, will yuh?"

Jan suddenly found that he was grinning up at the faces above him and swaggering down the steps. The boat was bobbing in the slight swell and, loaded as it was, the gunwale was none too far above the water. The guard salors were ready with their weapons as though expecting anything to happen and rather surprised that Tiger took it so mildly. Evidently he knew some of them, thought Jan.

Suddenly he remembered his manners and stepped back so that Boli, fat and awkward, could enter the boat first. And, seeing that the guard was quite on the alert and that the boat was, after all, bobbing rather badly even in this glassy sea, Boli was nothing loath to have a hand all of a sudden even from a criminal.

Jan felt stirring inside him and was too frightened to think the matter through, afraid lest he discover another awful plot within him. He took hold of the bowman's boat pike and helped him hold the barge in to the landing stage.

Boli, striving to see over his chest ruffles, watched the barge drop four feet below the stage and then bounce four feet above it. In truth, the condition was very ordinary, seeing that there had to be some manner of swell about a vessel anchored in the road, but Boli had had one or two in the captain's cabin and he well knew that his reputation only wanted a ridiculous incident to throw down much of his carefully built authority.

"Here you," said Jan—or rather Tiger—to the gunwale guards. "Give m'lord the port captain a hand before I knock you about. Look alive, swabs!"

The two moved hastily, getting up on thwarts to reach for Boli's hands and steady him. They were going through a usual routine but the presence of Tiger had rather shattered their composure. Boli wished ardently that the vessel weren't so far to sea.

"Easy, now, m'lord," said Tiger, looming above Boli as a church steeple rears above its almshouse. "When she starts down, step aboard and lively. And you, y'landlubbers, don't muss'm up or I'll break your skulls like they was eggs. Now!"

He eased Boli ahead. The barge swooped down from the height of the port captain's head. Boli, aided by Tiger's left hand, stepped to the gunwale as it flew downward. His men eased him quickly aboard while the barge kept on going down to four feet below the stage.

Tiger, still holding the bowman's pike in his right hand to help the bowman hold the barge in, suddenly yelped, "Don't pull her in, you fools!" And pulled her in with a jerk which almost hauled the bowman out of the boat.

The next instant an awful thing thing happened. The barge, four feet under the stage, started instantly on its upward surge. But this time it didn't miss the underside of the protruding stage. With a rending jar, the gunwale caught under the stage itself and the wave did the rest.

With a swoop, the barge capsized! One instant it was a normal enough boat, full of sleek and flawlessly uniformed sailors and the next the only thing which could be seen was the keel, all dripping and bobbing on the waves. From tumblehome to tumblehome, the boat displayed its bottom.

"Help!" bellowed Tiger, safe and dry on the landing stage.

But before help could even start, sailors out of the barge were rocketing into sight all about it, having ducked out of the terrifying but perfectly safe air pocket under the boat.

Tiger waited to see no more. He went overboard in a long dive. The green water fled past him. The dark barge was over him. And just ahead was a pair of very fat legs kicking desperately. Tiger encircled them deftly and hauled hard. Down into the sea went Boli!

Tiger came up by the stage an instant later to let a wave boost him to a hold. Boli was floundering like a grounded whale but still Tiger did not let him be. Up he came and up went Boli to his brawny back. Swiftly Tiger made the deck, surging past the ship sailors who were fishing up the boat guard, man by man.

Laying the port captain out on a hatch cover, Tiger pumped him thoroughly dry, taking the weak but strengthening protests as unworthy of notice. Respiration seemed to work wonderfully upon Boli and in no time at all the man Tiger had rescued from the watery grave was sitting up turning the air scarlet and azure all about him.

The barge men were hauled up, every man of them, to be dumped in all postures by the ship sailors. There was no great love lost between seamen and the spying patrol which policed the port.

All the while Jan was shuddering in horror. If he was in trouble now, what would he be in in a few moments? But he was utterly powerless to do anything about it and he was aghast to hear himself say, upon Boli's running out of breath, "By God, m'lord, it's lucky I was there. If you'll take a sailor's advice, m'lord, I'd jail that bowman for a month, so I would. Why, by God, sir, even when I yelled at him to desist, he insisted upon hooking his pike into the stage itself and pulling you under it! Beggin' m'lord's pardon, but you'd better get some sailors in that crew of yours that know their business. Damned if not."

Boli glowered and had dark suspicions. Tombo and Malek tried to keep scowling and be severe. The sailors attempted to stifle their merriment until a more appropriate moment.

"Is your breath all right now, m'lord?" said Tiger with earnest interest. "Captain, perhaps he'd better be let to rest in a cabin, if I might suggest it. That was a very trying thing and though he came out of it like a hero—"

"Tiger!" said Tombo.

"Sir?" said Tiger.

Captain Tombo tried to scowl more ferociously. But it happened that he had, on many occasions, suffered great delay because of the effeminate whims of this gross port captain and, for the life of him, he couldn't carry that much sail at the moment.

"Tiger," said the captain with a glance at Boli. And he was about to go on when he saw the bedraggled silk which hung in bags all about the lord. He changed his mind.

"Sir?"

"Give them a hand in righting that boat."

"Yes, sir."

Tiger sped down the gangway once more, where the ship's mirth-convulsed seamen were working. They said nothing. They couldn't and still keep their laughter inside where it would not offend Boli's ears above. But their eyes were full of great affection.

They righted the boat and, shortly, Boli's guard came down, leaving a river of water to run behind them on the steps. Gingerly they got into the barge. Nervously they prodded Tiger into the stern sheets. Fearfully they aided the port captain to his seat of state amidships.

They shoved off and all along the rail above, sailors

waved farewell. Even Captain Tombo smiled and Mr. Malek put a rope-scorched hand to his cap and raised it slightly to call, "So long, Tiger. We'll all be in to see you."

Boli rolled around and glared at his prisoner. Now that the port captain was on his own deck, so to speak, he was quite recovered—save that his ribs ached from the respiration treatment.

"You are very clever, my fine bucko. Everywhere you set your foot, things happen. I have heard it. Well! Do not think for one moment that your saving of Admiral Tyronin from the Isle of Fire, that your timely bombs at the Battle of Barankeet, that all your other mad deeds will stand a bit in your favor. You have flown too high. Whatever these charges are," and he fished a sealed packet from his soggy shirt, "and I don't doubt that they are severe enough, you will be tried for the crime at hand, not for deeds of questionable character long past. You have been recommended for trial by the queen herself and if she doesn't sentence you to swing, it'll not be fault of mine."

There was so much hatred in Boli's voice that Jan shivered. Out of him, like a dying fire, went the reckless madness which had brought him to that deed just done. He could not reason that Boli's hatred was not only born of that deed but of another, more delicate thing. Boli was badly built, ugly beyond description. And above him sat a tall, handsome fellow of a rare kind calculated to stir the most frigid of feminine hearts. But Jan could not see himself. Jan was just Jan now. He recognized no ships, he recalled nothing. He even fumbled for his glasses to wipe them in his confusion and was mighty startled to find that he wore none—indeed, did not seem to need any.

"The queen?" he gulped.

"The queen," said Boli, satisfied now that he could feel the uneasiness in his prisoner. "Not four days past she put five heads on pikes outside her palace and that for mere thievery on the high-road. I am given to understand that you have some dread stigma attached to you. Ah, yes, my fine prankster, it seems that your light-hearted days are done. Before you there is nothing but doom and death."

Boli enjoyed himself for the moment and almost forgot how wet he was. For the remainder of the voyage across the harbor, he piled up torture and watched his victim squirm. But when he reached the quay, a number of loafers, beholding m'lord the port captain as soggy as a drowned rat, burst into braying mirth.

Boli swept an imperious eye across the rank on the dock and roared, "Sergeant, arrest them! Up, I say! I'll show you the price of laughter, that I will!"

And though his guard tumbled swiftly up the gangway, when they got to the dock, not a man was left. Only laughter's echoes were there.

Snorting, Boli stamped to the wharf while four men carried Jan along at the points of their swords.

SEVEN

Jan, bewildered, stared up at the buildings of the town. They stretched back across the plain for miles. They reached around the harbor for leagues. What an immense town it was! Commerce jammed the wharves. Men sweated and swore, hauling cargoes about. Horses stamped and neighed as they strained at rumbling trucks. A bewildering array of signs spread out in every direction and the odd part of it was that one moment they were so many chicken scratches to Jan and the next their meaning was quite plain. Taverns and brokers' offices, sailors' hotels and shipping firms, trucking barns and chandler shops. Immediately beside them reared the customs, a building some four stories in height and of a queer architecture which was prominent in its immense scrolls and swoops and towers. All the buildings were like that, presenting a baffling line of distorted curves and garish, mismatched colors.

Along the docks bobbed fishing boats, small beside the towering castles of the ocean-going ships. From the scaly decks of the little craft a variety of weird sea-food was being hoisted, so that Jan knew it was still very early in the day.

Boli stamped away up the stairs to his quarters, where he could get a consoling nip and a change of clothes. His guard, forgotten, stood about, damply keeping an eye on their prisoner, very careful not to get within arm's length of him. Jan found quite accidentally that when he wandered along he carried the whole company with him and so, benighted as he was with woe, he strolled restlessly back and forth, the men moving with him but well away from him and all about him.

Jan stared down at a pile of flapping fish just tossed from a tubby little vessel's hold. He had never before seen any such denizens of the sea as these. Their eyes were lidded and winked and winked. They were as wide as they were long and their heads were as big as their bodies. For all the world they resembled sheep and Jan wondered distractedly if they tasted like mutton. Some of this catch was being laid on a miserable peddler's cart the wheels of which spread out very wide at the top and very narrow at the bottom, giving it a bow-legged appearance. Presently the two who had been loading it were accosted by the master of the fishing vessel who held out his palm for his pay.

One of the pair was a woman. Her hair was snarled beyond belief and a filthy, scaly neckerchief was swathed about her scrawny neck. Her dress glittered with dried scales which showed up very brightly against the black dirt which smeared the whole, shapeless garment. Her pipestem legs shot up out of hopelessly warped shoes and got no thicker when they became a body. She could have passed through a knothole with ease and, doubtless, such an operation would have taken a lot of the dirt from her. She chose to be niggardly about the price.

"You soul-stealing lobster!" she shrieked in a cracked ruin of a voice. "You—" Jan wanted to stop his ears. "Last time you charge two damins the feesh! This time you charge t'ree damins. We don't have to buy! We don't have to deal with the slimy likes of you! We'll take our trade elsewhere!" Her companion, an incredibly diseased fellow, tried to calm her. The fisherman tried to break in with the explanation—quite obvious—that these fish were especially fine, big ones. She would have nothing of it. Her rage mounted higher and higher, in direct ratio to the humoring it got from the two men. Finally this virago seized one of the fish by the tail and began to lay about her with all her might, screaming the foulest of language the while. Her rage made her blind and she lambasted several of the guards who could not get out of the way fast enough.

Jan was successful in ducking a swing but he tripped over a bitt and fell to stare up and get a full view of this termagant's ugly face. He recoiled, frozen with revulsion.

This shrew, this harridan, this screaming unholy catamaran resembled no one if not his Aunt Ethel!

He recovered and scrambled back. At a safe distance he peered wonderingly at the woman. The voice-tone, now that he listened for it, had a certain timbre; the eyes, the nose, the very ears carried the resemblance. Her build, the way she stood now that she was calming down in the wreckage of her victory, was also similar. And finally, though he could not understand how it could be, he was forced to grant this revolting creature the identity of his aunt. Aunt Ethel, wife to a diseased fish peddler! Aunt Ethel, bawling like a harlot upon the common dock!

But how on earth did she get there?

Now that hostilities had ceased and a lower price had been paid, the woman signaled to the man to be off and the two pushed the cart along toward the shoreward end.

"My darling Daphne," said the fish peddler, "the price we saved won't cover the cost of bandages for my head. By swith, how it rings!"

"Be quiet, you wretched apology of a man. I'll deal with you later when we get home."

But Jan had to know. He stepped forward beside the cart. "Aunt Ethel," he said, "how—"

She stared at him angrily and brushed on by, just as his guards leaped up to take him again and keep him from communicating with others. She glanced back in high disdain and snorted.

"Y'see? Y'see, you worm-eaten miscreant? I'm sunk so low that convicts talk to me! Ohhh, you wretch, if you think your head rings now—" And so they passed out of sight just as Boli, much fortified, hove like a barge into view.

Boli had a fresh company of Marids with him who swiftly and efficiently took Jan in hand.

"Take care," said Boli. "Your heads answer for it if he gets away."

A sedan chair was borne to them by four Marids and into its cushioned depths sank Boli. He raised his handkerchief and flourished it and the party moved off.

Dread began to settle heavily over Jan. What had possessed him to first frighten the wits out of a sailor and then upset a whole boatload of guard sailors, to say nothing of almost drowning the port captain, m'lord Boli? What unplumbed possibilities did this swaggering, brawny body of his contain that he had never before felt? And would he do something the very next minute to make his doom absolutely certain—if it weren't already so?

He was almost treading on the heels of the last two chair bearers. And suddenly it occurred to him that all he had to do was take a slightly longer step and into the street m'lord Boli would go, perfumed handkerchief and all. Ah, yes, and just ahead there was a lovely, wide mud puddle where horses had been tethered not long before. What a bed for m'lord Boli that hoof-churned muck would be. Just a slightly longer step and—

"I won't!" yelled Jan.

M'lord turned around in astonishment. "What was that?"

"Nothing," said the miserable Jan.

On they marched and finally negotiated the mud puddle. Jan sighed with relief when they got to the far side and on dry pavement once more. He took courage at that. It seemed that a sharp exertion of will power would cause this Tiger to fade away. And God knew that one more misstep would put m'lord Boli into an even higher howl for his blood.

He took an interest in the town and found that the mixed lot of the population was very, very unbalanced where wealth and position was concerned. Ifrits were to be seen at rare intervals and each time they were being borne in splendid carriages which were, invariably, driven by humans in livery.

Too, the silken robed proprietors of these great stores, when seen standing outside, were all jinn. Although human beings were not without some small finery here and there, not one actually wealthy one was to be found. The police were all Marids, resplendent in green cloaks and towering, conical white hats. Marids did not seem to be servants but monopolized all the minor positions of responsibility.

Here and there men turned to gaze after the marching guard with curiosity. Sometimes men saluted the port captain and he daintily waved his handkerchief back. Sometimes Marids held up traffic to let the procession through and then glowered ferociously upon the prisoner as he slogged past.

Once or twice people yelped, "It's Tiger!" And gaped helplessly until the company was out of sight. Jan recognized them but didn't recognize them. One he knew for sure was a tavern keeper on the water front. The other, a buxom female, he knew not at all. He was afraid there were tears in her eyes.

Far ahead, shimmering in the heat, Jan could see a large square opening out. It was easily a mile on the side and parked trees inclosed a great lake. Too, there were barracks and a parade ground, and, set far back, was a low, domed edifice which was deceptive. It appeared to be a normal building at first, done with the usual swoops and curves. But the closer one got, the bigger it got until, from across the huge square, it had the proportions of a mountain. The dome was seemingly solid gold and the sun on it made a man's eyes sting. The balconies were evidently masses of precious stones—or else they were all on fire. The fountains, which geysered so brightly before it, went a full hundred feet into the air and even then did not reach a height as great as the top of the steps in front—steps down which a cavalry division could have charged with ease.

Humans began to be less and less in evidence. This park was evidently the haunt of military men, all of them Marids, except the officers who were Ifrits. Their gaudy uniforms fitted them loosely, held close only by sword belts. The men were in scarlet and the officers too, except that the Ifrits had a great, golden bird of prey on wing across their breasts and three golden spikes upon their shining helmets.

Coming away from the palace was a small party in azure. They, too, had golden birds upon their tunics, but from the roll of their walk and the curve of the swords at their sides it was plain that here was a party of naval officers on its way to the harbor.

Coming abreast of the group, Jan glanced wonderingly at them. He had not yet gotten used to seeing fangs glittering in each jinni's face and these fellows looked especially ferocious. It almost startled him out of his wits when one, more fearsome than the rest, cried out in a voice which bespoke a mortal wound.

"Tiger!" cried this Ifrit. And then, tearing his luminous orbs away from the man, he held up an imperious hand. "Stop, I'd speak to your prisoner."

"Come along!" m'lord roared at his guard. "Commander, you speak to a royal prisoner. Have a care!"

But the guard couldn't very well walk straight over a commander in the navy, and as the commander had stepped in close to Jan, they had to stop. Boli raged.

"What's this?" said the naval officer. "By the Seven Swirls of the Seven Saffron Devils, Tiger, what are you into now?"

"Come along!" roared Boli. And to the officer: "Sir, I'll have your sword for this! I tell you he's a royal prisoner and not to be spoken with by anyone. Answer him, prisoner, and I'll rip out your tongue with my bare hands!"

"Shut your foul face, lover of slime," said the officer. And to Jan: "Tiger, I told you that if you got into trouble to come to see me. This confounded law which makes it impossible for you to have rank of any kind has got to be changed! You wouldn't revolt if you had any status. What's up?"

"Damn it, sir!" cried Boli, leaping out of his sedan chair and waving the handkerchief like a battle flag, "get back before I'm forced to order a stronger means!"

The officer, knowing well he was out of bounds, fell back slowly, looking the while at Jan. "Don't forget, Tiger. If they don't let you go, send the word and I'll be up here for you with my bullies if necessary. We haven't forgotten what you did for us on the Isle of Fire."

But the guard was moving off and Jan was pushed along with them. He was dazed by being known by men he did not know. And suddenly it came to him that now was the time to trip those bearers. Out went his foot, but in the nick of time he tripped himself instead of sending Boli hurtling down the steep steps.

"Come along," snarled m'lord, all unwitting of his close squeak.

Jan, breathing hard and thankfully, made haste to pick himself up and follow.

They went through two immense doors, guarded on each side by silver beasts which towered fifty feet above them. Like ants they crawled along the polished floor of a hall which could have berthed a frigate with ease.

Ahead, two doors so tall that the neck cracked before eyes could see the top of them barred the way with their black bulk, and before them stood a crim-

son line of Marids, larger than most and leaning now upon silver pikes.

The chair bearers stopped. The guard stopped. Boli raised himself importantly. "M'lord Boli, captain of the port, with a prisoner to be thrown upon royal clemency!"

"M'lord Boli," said the major of the guard, "enter."

The great doors swung back without, it seemed, any hand touching them, and between them stalked the company.

Ahead, Jan saw a white throne rearing up thirty feet from the floor, hung with tassels of gold and set with diamonds. Behind it, full fifty feet across, hung the great scarlet flag with its golden bird spread upon it.

The hall, which could have housed the biggest building in the town, was peopled scatteringly by brightly clothed courtiers and officers.

The blaze of the throne was such, under the onslaught of the sun which poured through the wall-sized, stained-glass windows, that Jan could not see the person in it. But as the procession drew near he was startled to find two lions chained with silver at its base, lions as large as camels, who eyed the approaching Boli with wet chops and licked their lips over the prisoner as an afterthought.

Above them reared the throne itself, and Jan, blinking in the blaze, beheld the queen.

She was taller than these other Ifrits. Taller and uglier. Her arms were matted with black hair which set strangely against the soft silk of her white robe. Her hairy face was a horror, her lips spread apart by upper and lower fangs like tusks. On either side of her jeweled crown were black, pointed ears like funnels. Her nose was mostly nostril. Her eyes were as big as stewpans and in them was a flickering, leaping flame which scorched Jan to his very soul.

He looked down, unable to stand the blaze. He looked down as he marched nearer behind m'lord

Boli. He looked down as the last two sedan bearers topped the double step which surrounded the throne. He looked down and saw their *heels.*

Suddenly there was nothing he could do about it. As he mounted, himself, he lurched a trifle. With horror he found that he deliberately caught at the scabbard of the guard on his right and—oh, quite accidentally—lifted it between the legs of the carrier.

The bearer lurched. His comrade, thrown out of step and balance, lurched. The two men forward, feeling the chair go back, surged ahead just as the two in the rear also strove to stop the sudden motion.

Crash! And down went m'lord Boli in a heap of howling guards. Shot, he was, like a catapulted rock straight out of his chair and directly between the huge lions!

There sounded a concerted scream in the hall. The guards, falling this way and that, had no time to see the horrible death which was even now bending dually to scoop up their fat morsel of a master.

But Tiger!

He leaped over the sprawling men. He charged up the second double step which put anyone in reach of the giant beasts. And the very instant the mouth of the first opened to gulp Boli's trunk down raw, the mouth of the second was gaping to finish the other half.

But Tiger!

He leaped astraddle the port captain and let out a mighty roar. With his left hand he smacked the left-hand lion resoundingly upon the nose. With his right hand he almost pulled the long tongue out of the mouth of the right-hand lion. And when they jerked back in astonishment at such audacity, back leaped Tiger, hauling Boli swiftly by the baggy seat of his lordship's pants.

Tiger lifted Boli to his jellied legs and made a great show of dusting him off, though the crack of the dusting was unseemingly loud.

"Your royal majesty!" cried Tiger. "You'll please forgive this man's clumsy antics. He feeds his bearers on very bad rum to make them trot the faster, and it's the quality, not the quantity, of the fare which made them stumble. I swear, your royal highness, if the smugglers in your royal realm don't stop paying off your lordship, the port captain, in such filthy bellywash, they'll be the death of him, as you can very well see! Are you all right, sir?" he said solicitously to Boli. "Ah, yes, not a drop of grease on the outside and so no fang struck home. By the way, your royal highness, I happened to be a prisoner of the port captain here, and I think he is very anxious to get on with his business of having my head and so, pray, give him leave to speak. There, m'lord, talk up, talk up and don't keep the noble jinni waiting!"

Boli had up enough pressure in him to splatter himself all over the hall. But such was his terror of the queen that he suddenly lost his rage, vowing that Tiger's death would be none too quick to suit him. He took a grip on his vocal cords and though, when he tried them out they squeaked alarmingly, he strove to hold forth.

"Your royal highness, I know not the crime of . . . of . . . this . . . this—"

"It's the lions," said Tiger helpfully. "They breathed too much gas into him. Go ahead, m'lord, pray cough up the letter my captain gave you."

A slaying scowl swept over m'lord's fat face, but forthwith he dug out the sea-worn message and, via a courier whom the lions considered indigestible, gave it to the queen.

Her black-haired hands wrapped about it so that their curved talons clicked against one another. She looked for some time at Tiger and then broke the seals. She read with great attention, and then with growing alarm. She had been, when Tiger tripped Boli, on the point of uproarious laughter, but now thunderclouds settled over her visage and her great round eyes flashed lightning.

"Has he spoken to anyone, you bungling clown?"

Boli shivered so that waves went through him like a shaken pudding. "N-n-no, your royal highness. Only . . . only a fish peddler's wife."

"What's this? What's this? Find her. Find her at once and throw her into the dungeons for observation. Oh, woe take you, miserable milksop! A goat could run my port the better! Did not his captain charge you with the seriousness of his detention? Had you no idea of the enormity of the trust given into your hands? Doddering imbecile! Go wave your stinking perfume in the faces of the water-front harlots and take the stain of your filthy boots from my polished halls! Begone!"

At the voice which made the whole gigantic room shake, Boli shook as a tree in a gale. He backed hastily, tripping over the double step, falling against some of his men and then, more swiftly, backed at express speed with his guard clear across the hall until the great black doors clanged shut in his face to blank him from view.

"I ought to have his head," snarled the queen. "I, Ramus the Magnificent, to be served in such a chuckleheaded fashion!" She fixed her eyes then upon Jan, who, quite empty of any Tiger now and only aware that he was asking for death if he so much as blinked, stood with bowed head before her. She grunted like a pig and then made a motion toward her guard with her heavy gold scepter.

"Take him away! Put him in the strong room in the left wing and let no man speak to him, human or jinni. And you, general, as fast as horses can travel, as fast as ships can sail, bring me that vile trouble maker Zongri!"

"Zongri?" ejaculated the general. "You mean Zongri of the Barbossi Isles? But how is this? Thousands of years ago—"

"Silence!" roared Ramus the Magnificent. "Bring him to *me!*"

"Your royal highness," said an espionage agent, stepping slyly forward, "this Zongri but yesterday arrived here in Tarbuton. I know where he is to be found."

"You serve me well. Go with the general and show him the way. I must have that fool!"

"Your wish is our law, your royal highness," said the general, backing out.

"Commander, you know the ship of Captain Tombo?"

"Yes, your royal highness," said the officer.

"Take him a suitable present for service so discreet. A fine present. See the treasurer."

"Yes, your royal highness."

She sank back on her throne with a worried scowl and then, glancing after the guard which escorted Tiger away, growled something to herself and burned the message in the incense cup at her elbow.

Jan, backing perforce, did not miss the gesture. God, he groaned, it's as bad as that. Damn the day I first set eyes upon that copper jar!

EIGHT

The strong room depended, mainly, for its strength upon its extreme height from the ground. It was no more or less than the topmost room in a turret so lofty that it was not unusual for clouds to obscure the earth of a morning. But Jan had seen too much of late to be so very amazed with the furnishings of the place or at the fact that it was very strange to be imprisoned in such splendor.

Money was no fitting measure for the furnishings. On the floor, to soften the alabaster, lay great white rugs of wool, thick as soup tureens. The walls were covered with shimmering cloth of gold into which amazing battles had been deftly worked. A sergeant could have drilled a squad on the bed, and a bos'n could have bent a mains'l on the posts. This last occupied the center of the room and a circular series of steps surrounded it, making it into a sort of fort of its own. All around the walls ran a ledge so softly cushioned that a man could quite easily have drowned in it and, instead of chairs, chaise longues of a graceful pattern stood face to face and yet side by side so as to offer easy means of conversation.

The scarlet-clocked Marids posted themselves on the landing outside and bolted the door with twelve bars of iron, flattering even the strength of Tiger's brawny body. Disconsolately Jan wandered through the room. At one side a silver staircase spiraled steeply up through the roof and, thinking he might find a way out, Jan mounted it and thrust back the trap at the top. A gale almost blew his hair off, but he went on through to find that he stood upon the highest level of the palace except for the golden dome itself and he was almost even with that. The platform itself was hardly like an ordinary turret top. The floor was mosaic and the parapet was all green tile. Seats were handy at every side but Jan was interested more in escape than scenery.

Going to the edge, he leaned hopefully over. He recoiled at the height. Below, a squad of men were red ink dots on the pavement. But he did not give up. Around he went, examining all sides of the hexagonal structure, but nowhere did he find the slightest semblance of a ladder, nor did he think he could have navigated it if he had. He sighed and walked back toward the trap; but, now that he knew escape to be impossible he was willing to give some small attention to his prison roof and he was somewhat startled to find, all about him, mounted astrological instruments of a pattern extinct these thousands of years. They were all in gold and silver and pivoted on glittering diamonds and so delicately balanced that the slightest touch on the mother-of-pearl handles swung them swiftly, and yet a slight turn of the same handle fixed them instantly.

Jan was instantly taken with the beauty of an astrolabe on which were engraved fanciful representations of the zodiac. The *rete* he noticed with a start, gave a very creditable star map, not at all antiquated, for it showed Polaris as the North Star. Until that instant he had supposed himself dropped back a few hundred years, but no! Polaris was its modern one and one fourth degrees from true north! From a very pretty object this astrolabe became a vital part of his life. He thought hard for a moment, recalling the sun's position for the date, and as he paced about he beheld a large chronometer under glass. He had all the data he needed. He swung eagerly back to the astrolabe and measured the sun's place in the zodiac and turned the *rete* until the position matched the circle on the plate's observed altitude. Quickly he made a line from that point to the circle of hours on the outer edge, holding his breath lest the answer be wrong.

What madness was this? It was his own Today, the Today of the Earth! There was the sun and here was the time. He was bewildered, and wandered to the parapet again to gaze out across the square miles of roofs to the bay where corbitas rubbed fenders with seventy-fours. He looked down at the patrol walks where soldiers marched with ornate, inaccurate old muskets. It seemed that all the bric-a-brac of antiquity had come home to Tarbuton like driftwood in the tide or like the mysterious tale of the Sargasso Sea. This place was heir to the glories of yesterday and yet was astonishingly very much in today!

Again he eyed the astronomical instruments as though they might have lied to him. Their glitter had originally been such that he had overlooked a perfectly good eight-inch telescope which stood regally in their midst. Before it was a small platform, cushioned with weatherproofed goods wherein the observer could take his ease and his science simultaneously.

Jan got into the seat, determined to inspect the town and possibly ferret out any modern touches. Evidently the instrument was used for this at times, as it had no fixed focus. He wheeled it down at an angle and trained it on the streets to wander the thoroughfares in comfort. Frenchman, Irishman, Jew and Hindu. Englishman, Russian, Chinaman and Greek. Nubian, Indian, Carib and Spaniard. White man, brown man, yellow man, black man. Every nationality was there, strangely clothed but unmistakable of face. Pulling carts, sorting bales, buying food and running errands. Loafing and sweating and gossiping and weeping. Laughing and drinking and swearing and dancing. Millions of them! Women sun-bathing upon flat roofs. Thieves dividing their loot in dark alleyways. An Ifrit beating his insolent slave. A money lender wailing outside his shop while a robber scurried unhalted down the amused avenue.

What a wild panorama it was! All the vices and pleasures and bigoted zeal, all the love and hate and sophistry and hunger. All the hundred-odd emotions could be seen raging up and down those broad thoroughfares or upon those wide roofs, in the shanties and the ships and the tavern yards, in the stores and courts and funeral parlors, and there was but one constant in it all. Emotion! Things were happening and life was fast and violent.

Strange were the mosques with their crescents originally been such that he had overlooked a per-rising up between a crossed steeple to the right and a pagoda tower to the left. Strange to see an idol with a dozen hands serenely surveying a court while just over the wall lay the dome of a synagogue.

Jan swung the telescope slowly across the garish scene and found himself gazing upon a towering hill, all alone in the plain. A temple, massive and plain, was sturdily square against the sky, and the broad, steep steps were blazing with the robes of the worshipers, going and coming. Jan discovered that they were all Ifrits, served by Marids, and that not one human being accompanied them farther than the lowest step. But wait, there were humans atop that hill. He focused the telescope better.

A long procession was just then starting out from the great entrance. A huge gold coffin all draped in white was being borne by human slaves, each one clothed in the livery of mourning. Before went a priest of the jinn bearing a golden bird a-wing at the top of a tall pole. Behind came a naval ensign and a personal flag. This was the funeral of some officer, it seemed, for here came the uniformed sailors with weapons all reversed. And following them were men in blue with golden birds upon their breasts and shining swords at their sides, the hilts turned away from their hands.

Then, from the balustrade Jan saw a hundred human girls step forth, each one with a basket of petals, to strew them under the marching feet as though the dead came as a conqueror and not a corpse. Humans, then, were servants of the temple, for all these girls were clothed in white robes, the hoods of which were thrown back to display a dozen different shades of hair.

Jan ran the telescope along the line of them idly. Suddenly he stopped and swiftly adjusted it again. His eyes grew large and his face paled. For there in the midst of those beauties was Alice Hall!

He could not mistake her, though she was more lovely than ever and without any care at all about her. Her robe, like the others, was slit from hem to knee, and her graceful feet arched as she walked down with the procession.

"Alice!" shouted Jan, leaving the telescope. But, instantly, the temple drew back three miles across the plain and not even the glittering coffin could be made out with the eye. When he looked again he had lost her.

"You called?" said a voice behind him.

Jan whirled as though to defend himself, but he relaxed on sight of the very old jinn who stood there in the trap. The fellow had gentle, mystified eyes, and his fangs were long departed. His claws were cracked and yellow and his hair was silver-gray. Upon his head he wore a very castle of a hat which was wound round and round with cloth that bore astronomical symbols.

"You have taken an observation, I see," he sighed. "I trust that the fate you found was not too unkind."

"The fate?" said Jan, climbing swiftly and guiltily down. "Oh . . . yes . . . no. I was checking your time." And he motioned toward the chronometer.

"It loses a second every day," sighed the ancient astrologer. "But tomorrow is a great event. It returns exactly to its accuracy and my computations will be the easier therefore." He looked and sounded too tired to live, as perhaps he was. "So many, many computa-

ASTRO
Year 1939
EDD CARTIER

tions. Every morning for the queen. Every evening for the lord chamberlain. And fifty times a day when questions come up. If"—he hesitated—"if you've already cast up your fate, you know, you might save me some calculations. I dislike prying into a man's birthday. It's so very personal, you see."

"I must confess," said Jan, "that I didn't, really. I only checked the time."

The ancient one sighed dolefully. Finally he got out a pad and began to request the data he needed. Jan gave it to him, and the modern dates and hours did not at all startle the old fellow. At length he shuffled over to his instruments and bent his watery gaze upon the star tables which were engraved on silver. For a long time he leaned on the tablet, scribbling now and then but sighing more than he scribbled. He advanced to the astrolabe to check his zodiac from force of habit and then, sinking down upon a bench beside a desk, pulled forth a volume half as big as he was. Jan helped him open it and for a long time the old fellow pored over magic writing.

Until then he had been weary unto death, but now, of a sudden, he started to take an interest in life. He read faster and faster, turning pages as leaves dash about in a hurricane. He leaped to his feet and sped to the star charts anew. He faced Jan and fired a very musketry of questions. Yes, the dates were right, but what on earth was wrong? But the ancient one, bobbing about now like a heron after fish, threw himself down upon the book and ate it up all over again.

Finally, sweating and almost crying, he leaned back, dabbing his forehead with a handkerchief all embroidered with suns and moons. He looked wonderingly at Jan, and Jan grew very uncomfortable. The astrologer's glance became more and more accusing and slowly the weariness seeped into him once more.

"What is wrong?"

"She'll laugh at me," he mourned. "More and more

they laugh at me ever since the day I said Zongri would make trouble within a year. They said he was dead these long centuries. But no. He is not. An hour ago he was hauled into the audience chamber by the battered guard which took him in the town. They laugh at me just the same. It was a terrible error for me to guess that Lord Shelfri would be kind to the princess. It is that which makes them laugh. Yes, it is that. He killed her, you know, and then hanged himself just last month, and so now they laugh. And they'll not believe me now. It is not possible. No human being could do such awful things in a land of the jinn. It is impossible and yet I must tell them."

"What must you tell them?" cried Jan.

"It is for her ears alone. And if she laughs and refuses to execute you while she has the chance, then it is Ramus who must suffer the consequences. It is all the same to me. I am old. I have seen the universe turning, turning, turning for a hundred thousand years. I weary of it, human. I weary of it. You, lucky child, will probably never live to see the sun roll across the heavens more than a dozen times more."

"You mean . . . you've read my death there?"

"No," he sighed. "No, not that. There is no certainty. I shall not alarm you. You may die. You might not die. But what does it matter? If you do, it is you who will lose. If you do not, the lives of many jinn will pay the toll. But I am old. Why should I care about these things? Ah-h-h, dear," he sighed, rising. "And now I must go down all those stairs again and give my report to the queen."

Jan followed him down to the room below, helping him on the steep stairs. But before the old man departed, he looked all around and shrugged as if seeing all the folly of the universe at once.

"It is not often this happens, you they call Tiger. While you yet breathe, rejoice. This you may or may not know is the strong room, and it is strong not to detain the visitor but to protect the queen."

"You mean . . . it's her room?"

"At times, when the nights are hot, she comes here to have read to her the fortunes of her people and her reign. That, you they call Tiger, is the bed on which Tadmus was murdered, on which Loru the Clown was stabbed to death by his chamberlain, in which lovely Dulon died in giving birth to Laccari, Scourge of two Worlds. Ah, yes, you they call Tiger, the whim of a queen has placed you upon an historic bed. Why, I have read in the stars. God save us all!"

And so he was let out and wandered down the steps sadly shaking his grotesquely hatted head, his mutters lingering long after he was gone.

Jan looked with horror at the great bed. And then, despite everything he could do to hold himself back, he leaped up the steps and landed squarely in the middle. He bounced up and down.

"Not bad," said Tiger.

"Stop!" cried Jan.

"Oh, boy! All we need is some dancing girls and a keg and what a time we'd have!"

"How can I think of such a thing at a time like this?"

"Hell's bells, why not? A short life and a hot one and let the devil have a break. It's not every day he gets such a recruit as Tiger."

"Blasphemy from *me?*"

"And why not? Why not, I say? Where's the idol tall and mighty enough to be revered? Where's the god or ruler strong enough and good enough and clever enough to get more than a passing glance from such a fellow as I? Not that I am worth a hiss in hell but that all these other pedestaled fools rate but little more. Show me a good god, a true king, a mighty man and all my faith is his for the asking—nay, not even for the asking. Who am I to be bowed by anything? Not Tiger!"

"But the queen and the God that made you—"

"The queen is a filthy harridan, and I have yet to

meet the God that made me. I am Tiger! I am Tiger, son of the sea, brother to the trade winds, lover of strength and worshiper of mirth! I am Tiger and I know all the vices of every land! I am Tiger and with my eyes I have seen such sights as few men so much as dream about. Dancing girls, honey-sweet wine, music, enough to tear the soul from a man. Aye, women to blind you with their golden eyes and flowing bodies. Aye, rum which mellows the throat and roars in the guts. Aye! Violins and drums, trombones and harps and feet so swift and so sure that the head whirls to follow them. Dancing girls!

"Aye! Such a one as graced the last steps of Captain Bayro with fresh roses this very day. Ah, for her I would crush this kingdom with my fingers and give it to her upon a diamond dish. Where has she been that I have not seen her? Where has she kept that sweet ankle and those silken curls? Where has she hidden that mouth made for kisses and laughter and songs? Ah, yes, the Temple of Rani. The Temple! Where no human dare tread save as a temple slave; where all Tarbuton's mighty go to babble their sins and kiss golden feet and win support for their hellish endeavors. The temple! Where the great horns bellow like bulls and the flying feet of the dancing girls sweep the worshipers into drunken stupor. The finest beauties of the realm to beguile the jinn with dancing. And that one, ah, the finest of them all! S'death to enter that temple. Death! But for the likes of that sweet mouth, for the slimness of that ankle—"

"Stop!" cried Jan. "She is sacred!"

"Sacred? Why not? All things of the temple are sacred. But though death might wait upon such a venture, if ever I get out of this mad palace, sure as the west wind blows I shall kiss that mouth—"

"She is sacred to me! To me! Her name is Alice Hall, the only woman I ever looked at. She is Alice Hall, the only woman who ever looked upon me with other than contempt. Seal your mouth and speak of her no more!"

"Sacred, you say? And why should a woman be so sacred as to never be touched? Surely now there's no reason in that at all! Love? For love I would lay down my split second of life. Love? Certainly I could love her, perhaps already I do love her. Yea, there's no use to deny it. Of all I've ever seen she is the *only* one. And what could be more sacred than to worship at that shrine? What could be more sacred than to burn the joss of desire before that cupid's bow of a mouth? Yea, that's given only to the strong. That's given only to the man-devil with courage enough to take it. Yea, she's sacred. Sacred to me! And as she is a temple girl, a dancing girl, raised out of sight of all humans, *I* shall be the first to plead with her. *I* shall be the last, for she will be mine! Now, puny and halting weakling, try and stop me!"

Jan leaped up from the bed, whirling as though to face an adversary. But no one was to be seen. And deep inside him he felt the Tiger stirring, heard the Tiger laughing. More and more as the hours passed he had experienced it. He had given it some slight leash on the ship and the musket had been fired. It had taken more, and the boat had overturned. And more and more to send Boli hurtling between two lions. And now, like the camel that stuck his head in the tent, slow degree by slow degree, presaging an end which might well be whole weeks away, he who contained the Tiger would be contained *by* the Tiger. And at such a prospect of being ruled by the lawless, pleasure-made irreverent sailor Jan recoiled with his own part of his soul. And even when he did it he heard the Tiger, far off, deep down, veiled and showing himself like the sharp fangs of a reef in the restless, heaving sea, laughing at him.

The body first, and then—then the heart? Who had the Tiger been? How had he become submerged at all?

And Jan in a spasm of terror would have thrown himself down on the bed anew if the door had not been flung back by a captain of the guard.

"Her royal highness, Ramus the Magnificent, now demands your presence in the audience chamber for trial!"

Jan stared dully at the pompous fellow and then obediently crawled off the bed and placed himself between the waiting files. They marched down the winding steps and through half a mile of halls and, with the greater part of him shaking at the prospect of the judgment, he could not help thinking that it would be a priceless joke if the Marid on his right should accidentally knock against the one in front. He was sure they would all go down like dominoes, so stiff were they in their glaring capes.

But the joke never came off, for the instant they entered the chamber Jan came up with a paralyzed gasp to behold Zongri, all in chains, standing on the steps which led to the throne. And Zongri was looking at him with eyes which were shot through and through with flashing fires of rage.

NINE

The audience chamber was clear of all except three companies of guards. The queen sat tensely regarding Zongri's back. Up before the throne the files marched Jan and then fell back to leave him isolated between two poker-stiff Marids.

The lions yawned hopefully, the sound of it gruesome in the echoing hall. As though that were a signal to begin, Ramus, the jinni queen, pointed her scepter at Jan.

"Speak, renegade Ifrit!" she ordered Zongri. "Is this the man upon whom you pronounced so untimely a sentence?"

Zongri shifted his weight. He was a tower of scorn and anger and his chains clinked viciously. "That one?" And he stared hard at Jan, a little of the resentment fading out of him. Jan held his breath, suddenly realizing that, in Tiger's form, he was not likely to be recognized by a jinni who had seen him but fleetingly and in bad light at that.

"That one?" said Zongri. "You mock!"

"Look well, jackal filth," roared the queen. "If he is not the one, you shall be detained until that one is found. And this one came to his captain with a strange tale indeed."

Zongri came down the steps a pace. He was above the reach of the great lions just as Jan was below them. And, framed between those tawny heads, Zongri looked more terrifying than ever, even though he did not seem quite so large as he had upon the first night. Even so, he was bigger than any one of the guards, bigger even than Ramus and certainly half again the size of Tiger.

Zongri's fangs clicked together as he worked his jaw in thought. Then he again faced Ramus. "You bait me! You try to trick me into lies! A trap worthy of you. The one I sentenced was a puny fellow, one these lions would have scorned to eat. A weakling with panes of glass over his eyes to protect them. A very owl of a scarecrow with his head stuffed with books and his heart so much sawdust. Try again, ruler of apes, for Zongri will not this time be led into untruth."

Jan's spirits began to pick up, and he even straightened his spine, and Tiger almost let out a merry whistle.

"Look again!" roared Ramus. "I tell you that this one brought such a tale to his captain and, though he is known as Tiger and though he is not unknown for certain brawling deeds, it is possible that he is not wholly the one you describe in form. Witless one, have you no eyes at all?"

"I," said Zongri in a voice like a file cutting through brass, "happen to be wearing your chains, Ramus. But my patience is great. For thousands of years I waited for my release. It taught me how to bide my time—"

"It taught you little else!" roared Ramus.

"But it *did* teach me that," said Zongri, looking as though he wanted to fly at her throat. "And I can wait until you visit me in my realm, the Barbossi Isles, where I would have been even now if your cursed ships were not so glutted with cargoes for the weaklings I find here. How am I to know what has happened in the ages since I left? How was I to know that the jest of eternal wakefulness, once so marvelous, would bring any danger here? How was I to know that soft living and slaves had reduced my race to the point of putty? My magic beyond my power? And if I have done this thing, what of that?"

"What of that?" bellowed Ramus in a fury. "You

witless son of chattering monkeys, can you not see the desolation which would spread if all humans in our world would come to know the *truth?* Quick now, stop blabbing your ignorance and closely look upon the prisoner. We must *know!*"

Again Zongri fixed his raging eyes upon Jan until Jan could feel them lifting off his scalp and tearing his clothes to ribbons. Suddenly Zongri tensed and took an involuntary step downward. Then, so swiftly that all his chains clanked as one, he faced the queen.

"If I can truthfully identify this man, you free me?"

"Of course."

"And allow me to depart?"

"With our most heartfelt relief!"

"Then, Ramus the Maggoty, know that the human before you is Jan Palmer, victim of eternal wakefulness and long may he roast in hell!"

Jan almost fell forward on his face but staggered upright again.

"Ah," said Ramus, "I see that the prisoner admits it, too. Very well, Zongri, we bear you no great malice—"

"I would that I could also say it," growled the giant Ifrit.

"—and will suitably see you away to your home."

"And no thanks earned," snarled Zongri.

"*If* you take away the sentence from this man!" snapped Ramus.

"Bah, why bother with that? Kill him and have it over!"

"Aye, that *would* be your solution, witless one. How like your sons you are, to choose the last resort first. This may be Jan Palmer, but it is also one they call Tiger, a man who earned a better fate by feats of daring in a dozen battles and who once saved the life of Admiral Tyronin, one of my finest officers. Certainly if it must be done, 'twill be done, but stay awhile. How, pray tell, were you able to put such a sentence upon him?"

"You said you would release me."

"I said I would, to be sure, but I had not stated all my conditions."

"You harpy!" screamed Zongri, leaping straight at the queen. Only the swift action of the officers on the steps kept him from reaching her. She had not so much as blinked and only smiled when Zongri was thrown back to his original position.

"We might forget to send you home at all, Zongri," she reminded him. "We have deep graves here for those who do not please us. Now, to business. We ask you to spare us the necessity of murdering this man, for, while your line has never done us anything but wrong, he at least has done us some slight good. To be very truthful, Zongri, we would much rather destroy you than this common sailor here."

Zongri was so angry he could not even speak. He cast the guards away from him and stood there, his ripped shirt showing a vast expanse of heaving, hairy chest. The other Ifrits averted their eyes from him but not inexorable Ramus. She was almost laughing to see such a powerful man so completely entangled at her whim.

"Come, speak up," said Ramus. "By what magic power did you bring this down upon Tiger? Speak! I would as soon execute you as not—in fact, I have no compunction whatever in the matter."

"I speak not from terror of your threats," growled Zongri, "but to avoid having to stay in such a treacherous place longer, gazing upon such ugly faces. Very well. You seem in this age to know nothing of the yesterdays. You know nothing or have completely forgotten the day when Sulayman brought us all to account by the magic which was his by virtue of his Seal." He seemed to doubt the wisdom of going on, but Ramus motioned for the executioner to step nearer and Zongri swept on like a rolling storm, his temper rising to white heat but telling his tale just the same. "Know that the Seal was lost to him some years after—"

"Come to the point. We have heard all that," said Ramus.

"It was lost to him and so was his power lost. You have heard of that Seal?"

"If you speak of the triangles laid so as to form a six-pointed star surrounded by a circle, we know the Seal of Sulayman." She chuckled to herself to see her guards wince at the mention of the potent thing.

"Aye," said Zongri, "such was the Seal. Such was the Seal of Sulayman and even a replica of it upon a leaden stopper carried sufficient force to entomb me all these bitter years, worn though it had become." He stopped again and stubbornly decided he would not continue. But once more the executioner stepped forward and once more Zongri blazed with the fury of impotence. "You have no right!"

"And you'll have no life," said Ramus. "It's all one to me whether we cheer you on your way or bury you."

"To Shatan with your threats. I speak to save myself further defilement."

"Then speak."

"When I was released, I touched the stopper as I said those words and, because the Seal was made by Sulayman himself and with that ring, there was enough power there to do it."

"You are not telling us the whole truth," said Ramus.

"Robbers, thieves!" shrieked Zongri.

"And what is that upon your hand?" said Ramus.

"Very well!" he screamed at her. "You'll have it all! I have shown great patience. I have tried not to destroy this city until I myself could occupy it with my own men, for conquest is my lot. But, abortively, my hand is called. Look!" And he thrust it forward.

She leaped back.

He jerked the ring from his finger. "Look! I searched but a day to find it. Sulayman got it back and I knew how to find his tomb. It lay in the miserable dust which remained to him, and I took it up and put it on and all the secrets of the two worlds will be mine! All the land will yield to me. Earth will disgorge her buried treasures, walls will fall at my bidding! Look well and be as stone!"

But nothing happened. Baffled, Zongri whirled around to face his guards. Again he howled the decree and still nothing happened, though he held the ring high over his head.

Ramus was the first to laugh aloud. "Oh, vain fool, in its life that ring gave all wisdom to Sulayman the Wise. But because it was worn by a human, it lost its power over humans. And now, think not that I know little of magic. *You*, an Ifrit, have worn that ring and so have destroyed its power there. Between you and Sulayman," she chortled, "you'll have it as powerful as a door-knob!"

"Beware!" howled Zongri. "Stand back. If it lacks that power, it still has many more. Stand back, I say!" And it seemed that only the lions would fail to obey as they strained toward him.

The Marids were so hypnotized by the strength of the man that they did as he ordered and, for the moment, Jan was standing quite alone, close beside the plate and iron which fastened the leash of the right-hand lion. Jan was sweating and then, suddenly, felt light-headed. Tiger grinned a wicked grin.

Down dropped Tiger to the floor and out of Zongri's wrath-blinded sight. It was the work of an instant to jerk out the confining pin. The chain had all the slack out. The lions were maddened by Zongri's loud roars, completely intent upon his dervishlike movements.

"See! I strike off my own chains!" shouted Zongri. And with a clank the enormous fetters dropped into a rusty coil about his feet. "And now, treacherous clowns—"

But the chain gave way in that instant and two thousand pounds of lion sprang straight at Zongri's hairy throat!

Zongri flung up his arms to meet the shock and staggered back. But Tiger was not at all idle. He went up over the beast's back, as if it were a ratline, and before two roars had gone shatteringly down the hall he was astride the brute's head and twisting his tender ears until they creaked like cabbage leaves.

It was a mad tumble of Ifrit, human and jungle king. So ferocious were the bellows coming out of the melée that the other lion, seeing them all hurtle down toward him, did not attack at all but leaped back in terror.

A dozen stout-hearted jinn officers flung themselves upon the chain and yanked the slack on it. Two more sent the pin clanging home where it belonged. A stout-hearted major dived into the mess and flung Zongri out of it and across the pavement. He grabbed again but the sailor had already leaped free, the lion lunging after. The chain pulled the brute back on his haunches and Tiger, seeing instantly that the devil was again chained, gave him a resounding cuff across his tender nose and snapped his fingers so hard that the beast started.

Complacently, Tiger stepped back between the two Marids who were still frozen in place.

Other guards picked up Zongri and lugged him forward to again stand him up before the throne, this time well clear of the lions.

"Ho-ho!" said Ramus. "Were you going to leave us so soon, Zongri? Stay yet awhile. Don't you enjoy the company? Major, take the ring away from him!"

That officer leaped up to do her bidding and yanked Zongri's hands toward him to remove the Seal. But, in a moment, the major gave a yelp.

"What have you done with it?" he cried.

But Zongri was obviously jarred by the discovery, for he jerked loose from the officers and scurried about the floor on all fours, searching. In an instant all the guards followed suit. Ramus watched them with a worried frown as though half minded to do some looking herself. But soon every inch of even that huge hall had been thoroughly searched without any result.

Zongri was the first to give up. "Your thieving guards have stolen it!"

"Sir, they are my personal household troops. Not one man of them would stop at laying down his life for me. Besides," she added, "my officers here have been watching them like hawks and I have been watching the officers. There were not so many."

"I demand that you search them all!" screamed Zongri.

"It shall be done," said Ramus. "Major, tell off three officers to do the searching. The Seal is too big to hide."

The searching was quickly done by the process of patting the capes of all Marids without result.

"And now the officers!" yelled Zongri.

"Even that insult I shall permit," said Ramus, "though I beg their forgiveness at such an affront. Major, search them."

The major, by the same process, did so and when he had finished, still without result, the voracious Zongri bellowed, "And now search the major!"

The officer disdainfully stepped up to Zongri and let himself be mauled, though his face had an expression as though he smelled something very bad.

"Are you satisfied?" said Ramus, troubled into mildness.

Zongri stared all about him, bewildered and growing angry to the point of insanity. Everyone in the room had been searched and the floor had practically been torn up and yet— With a sudden growl, Zongri leaped at Jan.

"You, you sniveling wretch!" cried Zongri. "You, the cause of all this! What have you done with that ring?"

Two officers started to intervene, but Tiger swept them back by throwing out his arms. "Search!"

Zongri would have ripped the clothes from him shred by shred, but the executioner was thoughtfully swinging his blade back and forth from the hilt and the glint of it slowed Zongri down. The patting process employed before was used now with such force that it almost broke Jan's ribs.

"This," said Tiger, "in payment for saving the ingrate from being lion beef. Search and be damned!"

Zongri ran out of pockets and patience at the same time and dealt Jan such a blow that he sent him skidding a full thirty feet across the glittering floor.

"Boor!" cried Ramus. "Haven't you done enough already?"

"It's a pretty show!" cried Tiger as Jan scrambled up. "I never saw a man work so hard to cover up a thing."

"What?" said Ramus on high.

"Why, 'tis plain as your horns, your royal highness. The fellow dropped it into that well he calls a mouth and gulped it down like pastry. Wasn't I within an inch of him when he did it?"

"What's this?" cried Ramus. "What's this? What's this?"

"You lying fiend!" yelled Zongri, making ready to leap at Jan anew. "You filthy-tongued—"

"Stop him!" ordered Ramus. "Ah, so that's the way it is, putting my most trusted troops to shame to pull a shabby trick. You'll learn my might yet, you snake-tailed donkey! Guards, put those irons on him, I say, and throw him into the darkest dungeon we have to offer until he sees fit to give us back that ring."

Zongri was swiftly overpowered despite his struggles and the irons rasped back into place.

"What about me?" said Tiger truculently.

"You!" roared Zongri. "Plenty about you! I'll hunt you down and rip out your throat if it takes me a thousand years to find you! You, you're doomed! Break your sentence, bah! It can't be done. Who excepting God, can destroy knowledge once given or separate personalities once fused? You, root of all my misery, will meet me in the realm of Shatan if not upon this land. Take me away!" he cried. "Take me away where I won't have to *look* at him!"

The guard was most obliging and Tiger laughed gleefully to see him go. And when Zongri had vanished Tiger faced the throne once more. "But that, your royal highness, still solves nothing. I, begging your pardon, am a man of action. Do I live or do I die? It's all the same so long as it's definite!"

Ramus leaned forward and spoke in a troubled voice. "Slave, your problem is not to be solved in a day. For the safety of my people I cannot let you free. For your service unto us I cannot have you killed unless you make it necessary. For the present, until your fate can be decided, I must hold you in the tower. Guards, escort the gentleman to his quarters."

A few minutes later the great metal door swung shut behind him and once more he was alone in the great room. But whereas before Tiger had always died out instantly after action and Jan had shivered and shrunk from the next event, there was now a difference.

It had grown dark long ago and someone had lighted an array of tapers in the diamond-pendant candelabra. By their flickering lights Jan made a quick but thorough examination of the whole room, scouting all places observers might be posted. Finally he yawned very elaborately, somewhat amazed at his histrionic powers. He pulled off his merchant sailor shirt and stepped out of his pants and then, clad only in his floppy-topped sea boots, he stepped over the candles and snuffed them one by one, yawning the while.

At last the room was dark except for the subdued light which rose up from the starry-lighted port. Jan crawled in between the silken sheets of the great bed, boots and all.

And then, secure, he reached into the floppy top of the right one and pulled forth a thing which weighed at least a pound. Even in the darkness the Seal of Sulayman blazed and crackled.

TEN

When the doze of an instant faded him from one scene to another, Jan, not yet used to the thing, failed to realize what had happened to him. Strangely enough he had the sleepy sensation of one who has spent a night of snoring. And so, without opening his eyes, he contentedly fumbled under his pillow for the blazing Seal.

It wasn't there.

In an instant he was on the floor turning his bed covers seven ways at once, making dust, oddments of clothes, books and cockroaches fly as from a bomb explosion. He got down on his knees and frantically fumbled with no more result than losing some skin from his knuckles. Up he leaped and plunged into the bed anew, ripping and rending it until it flapped like a flag on its hinges.

"What the hell's goin' on?" complained Diver. "You nuts or something?"

That brought Jan into a realization of his whereabouts. He stopped stock-still and then, like a cloud, the odor of disinfectant, unwashed feet and halitosis settled over him. Like a hum of bees the sounds of restless men came into his ears. Like a judgment he heard a bell tolling somewhere over the city, calling people to church.

It was jail, and it was Sunday.

And the mighty Seal of Sulayman was somewhere far away, in another bed, clutched in quite another hand.

Hopelessly Jan sank down upon the bunk.

"Geez, I thought you was goin' nuts for a minute. Not that you ain't already," he added with a sniff. "Now pick up that junk and make the place look decent, or I'll give you something to think about."

Jan glowered at his cellmate.

"Gwan, snap into it," said Diver.

For a moment more Jan stayed where he was and then a queer thing happened. With sudden alacrity he got up and made a great show of putting the cell in order. He had thrown things so far and so fast that they were now carpeting the place, scant though their number was. And Jan went at it with such a will that Diver was forced to stand up against the bars to get out of the way.

It was done in an instant and Jan stood back. "How's that?"

"Huh," said Diver, ambling back to his bunk and sitting down upon it.

Crash!

The astounded pickpocket was jolted through and through as his bunk gave completely away and slammed him down on the floor. He bounced up and gave the iron a resounding kick which instantly brought a yelp of pain out of him. Holding his toe he went hopping around like a heron and swearing like a pirate. Presently he subsided and frowning terribly picked up his few belongings and then, kicking everything out of the one remaining bunk, placed his own upon Jan's and took his seat there. He gave a growl as though daring Jan to do something about the theft, but Jan quite cheerfully picked up his own goods from the floor and put them on the wrecked bed and then, to Diver's suspicious amazement, reconnected the chain hooks, making the "wreck" quite as good as new.

"You done that on purpose," snarled Diver.

"Me?" said Jan innocently. "Why, you took my bunk and that leaves yours, so now yours is mine."

"Yeah, but this thing here isn't fit for a hog to sleep in!"

"Then why should you object?" said Jan complacently.

Diver eyed him doubtfully and seemed about to make a fight for it when breakfast appeared. Diver was too much interested in his stomach to put fighting before eating, and so he snatched the tray from under the door and put it on the table and, placing his arms about it, appeared on the verge of devouring it all himself.

Jan sat watching him for several seconds and Diver began to relax, throwing a scornful grunt in Jan's direction. Diver got his muscles in working order, snapped his teeth a couple times experimentally and fell to.

Jan still watched him. Two eggs vanished and the remaining two were about to follow the example of the first pair when Jan let out a startled exclamation.

"Look out!"

"What's wrong?" snarled Diver.

"Why, good golly, you wouldn't want to eat *that*, would you?" And he advanced, placing his hand close to the plate to indicate something.

Diver took his eyes off Jan and looked at the plate and there, squarely between the two eggs was the biggest cockroach he had ever seen! And not only that but only *half* of him was present.

Diver clapped one hand over his mouth and the other over his stomach, and his snaky eyes got big as dollars.

"Quick!" said Jan. "I've heard they're poison as arsenic. Guard! Guard!"

The officer, having distributed the last tray came speeding back. "What's the matter with you two guys now?"

"It's Diver!" said Jan urgently. "He's poisoned! Hurry, he may die even before you get him to the infirmary! Don't stand there gawking like an idiot! *Do* something!"

Jan swiftly aided Diver to the now open door, and the guard led away the staggering pickpocket, who still had his hands where he had first put them but now looked as green as a shark's belly.

"What's up?" said the counterfeiter urgently.

Jan yawned and watched Diver out of sight. Then he grinned. "It's something he thought he ate." And so saying he calmly sat down at the tray, chose clean tools and ate the ham and the toast and drank the coffee with very great relish. Tiger purred with contentment and the luxurious feeling which always follows a job well done.

The feeling of well-being, however, did not last very long. Jan, recalling Alice's present, stripped down and prepared for a shave. All went well until he confronted himself in the glass. With a shock he saw no one but Jan Palmer, thin and pale of countenance, narrow of chest, timid-eyed and, generally, about as unlike the handsome, swash-buckling Tiger as anyone could imagine. His physiognomy took the heart out of him. What chance did a miserable chip of a human being like himself have against the inexorable forces of the law, against the antagonism of his relatives, against a manager who would be only too glad to see him hanged? Weapons he had none. Friends he had none. Plans were as impracticable as they were nebulous.

He felt as though someone had drained the life blood from him, and he sank down upon the chair with a groan, blanking out the mirror with hands over his eyes.

"Oh God!" he whimpered. "Why, oh why, did I ever even hear of that copper jar?" He was silent then for a long, long time, and the patch of lather upon his face grew dry as cotton. At last he spiritlessly scraped the blond fuzz from his face and sponged himself in a vain attempt to dispel the penetrating odor of the jail.

It was only when he began to don the clean white shirt that he experienced a degree of relief.

Today was Sunday. Would she come to see him? Or did she, too, think he was wholly mad and only favored him as a soft-hearted woman feeds a mangy stray?

The day would tell that, might even answer all of it. And so he vainly attempted to speed the hours by reading Houdini. But as he found that absolutely none of the conditions for escaping set forth in the book were to be fulfilled in this jail and as the thought of getting out almost drove him wild, he at length gave it over and merely sat, listening to a tower clock strike the hours. Would she come to him today?

It was eleven, and then it was noon. It was one and the Sunday dinner was served with the information that Diver Mullins had been put to bed in the hospital after the exertions of a doctor and a stomach pump. It was two, and then two-thirty. And still no footstep like hers sounded in the hard cell block.

He gave her up and gloomily regarded a cockroach's attempt to climb the slippery side of the wash bowl. She wouldn't spoil her day with a visit to the jail. It was thoughtless of him to expect it. Besides, what was he to her?

"Well! What happened to your friend?"

Jan leaped a foot and came down standing. "Alice! I mean . . . Miss Hall! Gee, I . . . gosh."

The officer let her into the cell and locked it behind her. "I'll have to wait here, miss. I ain't really supposed—"

She beamed upon him, and he melted. With a heartfelt sigh he leaned against the bars and swung his keys round and round, beginning after a while to hum softly.

Alice put a package down on a chair and Jan seated her with such a flurry of activity that he almost knocked it off.

"You're alone today."

"Yes," said Jan. "Yes, I'm alone. Gee!"

She smiled at him. It was the first time she had done that and for an instant he was afraid that she might be amused by the way he acted. He sat down and became dignified on the instant.

"I . . . I didn't think you'd come. I almost gave you up. But you did, didn't you?"

"I thought they might not be feeding you well," and she lifted the wrapper off the box to show him a chicken and some swell rolls and a thermos of coffee and numerous other things which he couldn't take in all at once.

"Gosh, I mean you shouldn't do that." He floundered. "It . . . it cost . . . that is—"

"Oh, your uncle gave me the money."

Jan's face fell and then he brightened. "You're lying! Green wouldn't give a penny to his mother if she was dying of starvation!"

She squirmed, out of countenance for the first time since they had met. "It isn't much, really. I . . . I never have so very many places to put my pay. But please, let's not talk about that."

"Gosh, I'm glad he didn't," said Jan illogically. "But you shouldn't just the same, though it makes me feel swell to think that you would . . . unless . . . unless you do it just out . . . out of pity, that is."

She started. "How so?"

"Well . . . gee . . . I can't understand how a girl like you could . . . well . . . see anything in me."

"Don't, please."

"I've offended you, I know," said Jan. "I guess . . . I guess I'm not very good company. I'm sort of rattled, you see, and . . . and, well—Have you heard anything more about the bail?" he said abruptly to change the subject.

"I was at Mr. Green's home this morning to take some letters," said Alice. "And . . . well, none of them were about you. But I shouldn't talk like this because . . . well, it's sort of disloyal. After all . . .

but wait, I forgot. I always have to think hard to remember that you own the line."

"That's not much of a compliment," said Jan mournfully, "but I know it's well deserved."

"Well, then. Shannon came to see him and they talked for a long time."

"What about?"

"Mostly about Shannon's fee. He wants ten thousand dollars."

"To do what?"

"To keep you from being hanged."

"Then there's a chance I won't be?" cried Jan.

"Yes, of course there is."

"Wait. Look here. Do you believe me now? I mean, you don't think I did it, do you?"

"I don't know what to think. As for your story about the jinn—"

"But it's true!"

"Don't look at me like that," she said uneasily.

"All right. I'm crazy. Everybody thinks so and so I must be so. I'm crazy. I have strength enough in this toothpick of an arm to split a man from crown to waist. I have always acted crazy. I have hit people and shouted at everyone around the house—"

"Maybe it would have been better if you had. Look, Jan. Listen to me. Stop dodging behind that story and come right out and say it was self-defense. You've been reading too much, that's all. Come right out and tell the truth. After all it's a clear case of self-defense. Frobish came to steal that copper jar, thinking it might be full of ancient treasure. In his own field I understand the man was almost a maniac. Then, the odds are all with you. You had to kill him in self-defense, and I know that you had bruises on you—still have one there on your head, for that matter. He invaded your home and you were forced to threaten him and then he attacked you and you had to use that sword to save your life. A court will believe that. They'll let you go free unless—" She stopped.

"Unless what?"

"Unless what your aunt told the reporters will be used against you. And unless Thompson's statements, backed by Green, will influence justice. And if you have money enough to hire another lawyer besides Shannon."

"Their *statements?*" said Jan.

"That you were always violent at home and that, very often, they had to keep you out of sight so that the public would not know that the head of the Bering Steamship Corporation was . . . well . . . crazy."

"They said that?" cried Jan, springing up.

"Jan, if you have money you can get, I'll find the best lawyer in the country for you."

He sank down on the bed. "Money," he said dully. "I have none. What Green did with what I should have gotten I don't know. I thought he knew best and he said times were bad. I have no money."

"But at least you can use that plea of self-defense."

He gazed sadly at her. "A liar is always caught. I can tell nothing but the truth. An Ifrit named Zongri killed Professor Frobish and that is the only story I can tell because it is the only true one."

She spread her hands in a gesture of helplessness. "Then it is all over."

"Why?"

"Because if you tell that story to the judge tomorrow—"

"My trial is tomorrow? But how—"

"It's not a trial. On the recommendation of your aunt and Nathaniel Green and Shannon and on the findings of a psychiatrist who has already been paid five thousand dollars to do it, you are to be declared insane and sent to a private sanitarium from which no one can hope to escape."

"To a madhouse? Me? But they'll see there that I'm sane—"

"It's not their business to find anyone sane. It's a private home, far worse than any jail. I have heard of such places. They drug their patients continually, unknown to them, until at last they really are insane. No pardon board, nothing. Unless you change your story as I have told you, you'll be buried alive and Nathaniel Green will enjoy all the funds which he has looted from under your very nose."

"A madhouse," said Jan.

"No one will ever be able to see you and you know how they've visited you here. If you are declared insane—and it is as good as done except for the formalities involved—Green will automatically possess the power of attorney which you wisely refused to give him. The Bering Steamship Corporation and all that you own will belong to Green and your aunt. And at the sanitarium they'll kill you just as certainly as the sun will shine."

Horror crept into Jan's eyes. Nervously he began to pace up and down the cell and then, suddenly he gripped the bars and shook them, shook them until the echoes bit into every corner of the building.

Alice started back from him in terror. The officer quickly opened the door and pulled her out. And Jan, even then, did not calm himself.

"Thieves!" he shouted. "I'll show them! I'll show them!" And he beat his fists against the wall until the blood flowed from them.

In exhaustion he sank down upon the bunk and one hand fell across the box. Dully he looked for Alice and saw that she was gone.

"A living death in this world and who knows how long the other will last. And now I've lost the one thing in all this cursed universe that I ever cared about."

To wait would be his lot.

But at least, in another place, though God only knew where it was, he might manage to battle for some happiness there.

In a black mood he impatiently waited for night.

to the hypnotic power of her eyes which jangled with the hotness of the Seal of Sulayman which lay like a coal in his sash.

"You wonder who I am," she said.

He nodded.

"And why I have come here?"

Again he nodded.

She laughed and indicated the Marids who were now closing and bolting the door again. "Those fools. I wonder that as little happens as there does in this palace. It is so very simple to order them about and pass them by—"

"But they have orders that I am to speak to no one."

She laughed musically. "Do they? How funny. And yet I, who have no earthly business here, can walk airily through their ranks and into your presence as if they were so many dolls." The chamber awakened at her renewed mirth and the small glasses on the shelf above the bed hummed in gay sympathy. "Ah, now, but I am not mocking you. One would hardly mock Tiger, would they? You wish to know why I came?"

"Indeed I would, m'lady."

"How gruff! And, I might add, handsomely gruff. Mark it all to curiosity, my Tiger. All to that and nothing more except perhaps a fear that you were very lonely shut up here in this awful place and everyone ordered not to speak to you at all. You *were* lonely, weren't you?"

"Why . . . yes. Why shouldn't I be?"

She reached out her hand and took down two crystal goblets and a tall-necked bottle of amber wine. She poured them full and then held them up to the light to give him the one which contained the most.

"To the cheer of company," she toasted.

He was very acutely aware of the danger here, for she was the first human being he had seen about the palace, and he well knew that a woman would not be permitted to come here so easily, no matter how great her beauty. But when he saw that she drank, he po-

litely sipped his answer to her toast. His caution was prompted more by Jan than Tiger, for the wine was innocent compared to suddenly remembered beverages which went down with great authority.

"I am here," she said finally, "with a good reason. Now am I more welcome?"

"Welcome!" said Tiger abruptly. "If you've ever studied your lovely self in the most indifferent mirror, I wonder that you can still see. And you talk about being welcome." He clinked his glass against hers and drank it down.

With great difficulty Jan fought for the upper hand and again the Seal burned horribly against his side.

"I am here," she said, "to counsel you, for I am sure that in all the time you've found yourself in such a strange predicament not one of these thoughtless, witless jinn has thought to ease your mind about it. Ifrits," she added, "are really very stupid people."

"I have not found them so," said Jan.

"No? But you have not talked to them so very much, then. For they truly are stupid. You have no idea!"

"And what, may I ask, is your counsel?"

"Anxious to be rid of me? How can that be? But I had heard on great authority that Tiger was a gallant fellow, not to be denied. But, then, I forget, you may be mixed now with some strange personality from outside our crude world and perhaps you have an icicle or two on your ears." She looked and only found the ring holes in the lobes.

"Ah, a sailor indeed," she cried joyfully. "And what have you done with your gold hoops?"

"I pawned them," said Tiger suddenly. "Pawned them to buy a dancing girl a veil. I didn't want it but she did. And how was I to know that she belonged by rights to a captain of infantry and that he would enter the hall just as I was presenting it? You have no idea," he laughed, mimicking her.

"Gold hoops for a dancing girl!" she said, prettily

shocked. "How horribly wicked. And now you have neither dancing girl nor rings."

At the mention of rings, Jan fought to the surface. But the lady had jumped up and was detaching two hoops of gold from her girdle which she instantly spread and fixed in his ears.

"Now!" she cried. "Now you look like a true sailor."

"I feel like a very stupid one," said Jan, discovering cunning in his being. "How is it that I am here, shut up in an observatory tower when reason dictates that I should be in the deepest dungeon or else hanging on the highest gibbet in Tarbuton?"

"Must we have to do with reason?"

"Yes."

"Ah, you sound like the Tiger I have heard about. Never satisfied with anything. Here you are shut up in the queen's very own room, waited on by the finest of her servants, feasting upon the most palatable of food and with nothing to do but enjoy yourself. And you wonder about it!"

"Rather!"

"After all," she said, "I hear you once saved the life of Admiral Tyronin, among other things. And though your numerous escapades may make it impossible for you to be kept always on silk, the State owes you something."

"The State saw fit to put me on a stinking merchant tub."

"So?"

"With a stupid, flogging fool for a captain."

"Ah, that is sad. Perhaps the State feels you have been punished enough and wishes now to make amends."

"I am here," said Jan, "because of some strange information I might communicate to others. Information of which I confess myself wholly ignorant. If I am dangerous why doesn't the royal might do away with me and have done with it? I know very little about anything. I am a raw mass of questions. I know not even where this land is, though more and more I know my own deeds and misdeeds in it—as even now I recall certain other things I have done which might or might not have endeared me to the State. But I, who was one, am now two and I heartily dislike it."

"Two indeed. Brawling, laughing, drunken Tiger could never have taken a sight with an astrolabe."

"You know about that?"

"I am a very dear friend of old Zeno. Ah, yes, you are a strange blend now. I detect a scholar and philosopher in you, Tiger, things which go strangely with your clear brow and handsome strength."

"A scholar, perhaps. And little good it's ever done me," quoth Jan. "To do cube roots in the head avails a man little against prison bars."

"Scholars are scholars because they must fall back upon books to supply their lack in the strife of living. Scholaring, I am told, is a very dread disease. The more one knows the more one knows he knows nothing. And the more he knows that he knows nothing, the more ardently he desires to really know something and so, more study. And more study, the more he knows he knows nothing, the more—"

"M'lady, I beg of you, desist!"

"I was growing dizzy, too. But tell me, which of you has the upper hand. Scholar or warrior?"

Jan suddenly wanted to answer both at once and was strangely aware of some alchemy within him, by which he was losing none of the knowledge and memory of Jan but gaining the heart and courage as well as the knowledge and memory of Tiger. The nearness of this heart-quickening woman was completing the weld. He felt drunk.

"The question's a hard one," he said. "And perhaps I'd be able to answer it better if I knew what I was talking about. To begin, where am I?"

"Why, in the Kingdom of Tarbuton, of course."

"Oh, I know that well enough and I seem to know every alley and wall crack in the land as well. But I speak of geography. Am I fifty south and forty west? Is that sea the Mediterranean? And where is the United States of America in regard to this place?"

"Such weird names, my sailor. But certainly one who has sailed the world would know more about it than I. Not one of those places or numbers do I know." She brightened. "Why, can't you tell with old Zeno's instruments up there?"

"The astrolabe tells only of time and latitude. Zeno's time gives me no longitude and, though I suppose my reading of fifteen south might be correct, I doubt it very much because, you see that places us in the Amazon jungle, or the Belgian Congo, or among the head-hunters of New Guinea, or—"

"How many places there are that I have never heard the least bit about. Tell me of these places—especially about the head-hunters. Are they like ghouls, pray tell?"

"You've avoided my question."

"What an inexorable fellow! But how can I answer if I do not know?"

"You mean . . . you mean you've never heard of the United States or . . . or Africa or . . . or Arabia—"

"Ah, yes, I know that one from ancient history. Arabia! But that is far away and the route to it is wholly forgotten. Why, I dare say even one of our elders would find it difficult to discover Mount Kaaf in that world, much less the names you spiel so glibly."

"You're mocking me. Tell me the truth. Where am I?"

"Sweet sailor, in terms of your land I can speak nothing. I know them not. But lest I displease you I shall leave off this teasing and give you truth . . . truth as I have heard Zeno tell it. Here we call your world—your *other* world—the Land of Sleep. And perhaps your world calls this world the same—"

"Calls nothing. They do not even know about it. The Land of Sleep, you say?"

"Why, yes, that should be fairly plain. At least that is how Zeno tells it. There are two worlds of sleep or two worlds of wakefulness, whichever you will have. That is, so far as human beings are concerned. Human beings are weird people. Long ago we found that they had souls."

Every hair on Jan's neck was standing up straight. What was she doing, speaking of humans as *other than herself?* But, outside of knowing the pitfall which gaped to trap him, he made no further recognition, so badly did he wish to know more of his condition.

"I think I know something of this," said Jan. "The American Indian had some such insight. In sleep his soul walked from his body and visited another land."

"Yes, that is true. Long, long ago we found the Indian had to be very closely watched because of just that consciousness. Here and there others, or so says Zeno, have been vaguely aware of leaving their bodies when they slept, but it has become apparent—or was until you came here—that, so far as actual realization was concerned, these humans here know nothing of their other world—that other world of yours which contains all the strange names. And in their other world they know nothing of this world so that when they rest and sleep in either, they resume their second life in the other. Zeno says this leads to all sorts of silly dissemblances among the brighter humans here. They go about talking of 'double personalities' and 'split egos' and such."

"But . . . but how is it that the same man is so different in the two worlds?"

"That is pulling me in rather deep, my sailor, and you really should talk it over with Zeno. He could tell you all sorts of odd things about it and, truly, he is somewhat obsessed with his theories of it—perhaps because he never dares talk about them. Yes, you should talk to Zeno." She poured more wine and sipped at hers and then artfully changed glasses and drank of his.

"Don't you really know?"

"I hate to appear so stupid, and you are a scholar and might pick a flaw in what I say. I do not know that I speak aright. I can give you Zeno's theories but even those I know imperfectly. You see, your question is wrong. There really isn't just one man, or one soul, or one human. People, even the jinn—who are considerably less nebulously built and far less destructible, I assure you—consist mainly of a certain kind of energy. Some philosophers say that all energy is the same energy, but that argument is pricked by asking the question, 'Even if all energy is convertible into other kinds of energy does it follow therefore that life is convertible into other kinds of life?' And, of course, it isn't in the same way that a tree stores heat and then, when burned, gives off the heat again.

"We had a fakir here—quite a mad fellow by the way—who had somehow reached an ecstatic state whereby he merged both his souls into one—"

"Yoga! The Beda! The goal of the greatest cult in India! The attainment of complete Unity! And they say their souls go elsewhere and—"

"Well! Dear me, if you're going to become so excited and so disgustingly philosophic about it I shan't allow another word to be pried out of me, I assure you!"

"I didn't mean to offend," said Jan contritely. "But you see, all this explains the great mysteries of psychology and philosophy. And after all—"

"Oh. I suppose a man would be quite excited rightly enough. It is, after all, rather personal to him."

"You see, there is such a thing as dual personality, you know," said Jan more calmly. "A man may be a perfect saint and a perfect beast all in one body at different times."

"That's not so strange from what I've seen of men!" She drank and made him drink with her, and then, setting down her glass did not seem to find any further interest in the subject of dualism. Rather, the sailor himself had her eye.

"But don't leave me there," begged Jan. "You say a man's soul wanders between these two worlds—"

She sighed. "You have answered my question. The scholar has the upper hand. Oh, well," and she shrugged. "If I quiet the scholar, perhaps the sailor will come back. A man doesn't have just one soul—or so Zeno says. He has two souls and these work interconnectedly somehow. His life force—different from plain energy—is capable of only one focusing. He is either here or there and the world in which he lives forms the body which he has, and so, when one is awake the other is asleep. Brothers, you might say, across the Universe. It's a thing very difficult to achieve, this uniting of both in one body at the same time. And I dare say old Zeno might be interested in knowing whether you carry Tiger back with you to your other world."

"Tell me," said Jan. "How is it that you are so frightened here that humans might learn of this double world?"

"Sailor—please be a sailor, will you and not a graybeard?—there was once this fakir and there have been others. They were quite enough. Here all humans are slaves. This world is ruled by the jinn, it belongs to the jinn and always did and always will. Once human souls did not effect this change from world to world but merely wandered. There may be other worlds, too. How am I to know that? But, I say, human sleep souls wandered . . . where was I?"

The sailor was telling in him now. He pressed another drink upon her, himself not in the least blurry.

"Human souls wandered," prompted Jan.

"Oh, yes. And we were torn apart by the cursed wars of Sulayman against us. The jinn may live forever if they are not accidentally killed—though very few have ever escaped that, and Zeno is the only one I can call to mind who can remember things of a hundred thousand years ago—before humans were more than apes, it seems, or so he says. The jinn, I say, were torn by wars. There were not many and this land was large and bountiful and the jinn were unable to even maintain themselves upon it. Besides, neither jinn nor Marid enjoys manual work. And so, to ease the burden, several wise ones decided to carefully nurture a plan. It was easy, quite easy, to make bodies. But souls were quite another thing. . . . Where was I?"

He poured her still another drink and drank one with her. "The jinn made bodies—"

"Well . . . not exactly made them. To be frank, they stole them out of cemeteries in that world of yours. By enchantment they strove to bring them to life but it could not be done. And then some very bright fellows among us—I assure you they were very, very great magicians—snared these wandering sleep souls and made them come here. And as the days are of disproportionate length, though all is on the same ratio, the sleep soul was sixteen hours here and sixteen hours in its own world. It was no great trick to breed the trait into the race or to breed these revived bodies, made whole again by clever jinn surgeons. And so, there you have it.

"The jinn needed slaves and they got slaves, and we've had some trouble because some fellows here get very important and try to incite others with their discoveries. Usually we kill them, for when the sleep soul is trapped here, both bodies die and so we are spared. And so we have slaves. Lots of slaves. And we do them a great favor, too. Eh, sailor? Is this not a fine land? Is it not beauteous? And is it not a great, great pity that we cannot allow humans in their own world to know about it and, perchance, do something to stop it? What is so bad about slavery? We are generous. Right generous, I think. The soul here is the true soul.

Just as yours is the soul of a sailor. How unhappy you must have been as a scholar in your other world? I . . . uh . . . where was I?"

He poured her yet another drink and drank another himself.

Languorously she stretched. "Ah, but you're a handsome devil, Tiger." She smiled and moved closer to him.

Tiger smiled and reached out to put his arm about her. But suddenly, there was a terrible clamor outside and footsteps raced up the stairs, and all the palace reverberated with terrified shouts.

The woman came up straight and the door burst inward. Old Zeno, his towering hat askew and his robe all tangled in his rickety legs, stumbled to a halt.

"Your royal highness!" he cried. "Zongri—"

"You fool!" shouted Ramus, leaping to her feet. "You thick-witted jackal! What do you mean by this?"

Jan recoiled from her, for out of that comely shape rose the terrifying body of the queen, glittering fangs, matted black hair, split hoofs and ugly, scowling visage.

"Your royal highness!" quavered Zeno, not to be stopped. "This morning it was found that the pigeons of the royal Barbossi post had been missing for a day! And we have just found the dungeon guards all dead even to Captain Lorco! It's Zongri! He is gone and a swift lugger is missing in the harbor! Your royal highness! Forgive me, but the pigeons have long arrived in the Barbossi Isles and those cutthroat pirates will even now have crossed half of the channel. When Zongri meets them they will come back and we have but four ships of war ready for battle while they must have forty! Your royal highness, we're doomed!"

Ramus shivered. She hurried down the steps, hoofs clicking, to step to the seaward window and look to the horizon.

"Since morning?"

"Or since night!" cried Zeno. "It is the end of everything! My charts told you! I read them to—"

"Quiet, wreck of a jinn!" She rushed out of the room and as she charged down the steps, Jan could hear her bellowing, "Get me Admiral Tyronin! Withdraw the cavalry from their outposts! Officers! Guards—"

Jan dabbed at a very moist brow and Zeno looked fixedly at him.

"Well?" said Tiger. "You ought to be happy to have been so very right. It will put you up a mile or two around here."

"Laugh," said Zeno sadly. "Laugh, light-headed sailor. You have caused this. And Zongri is not returning to level this kingdom half so much as he is to find you and put you to the stake. God help you, blundering mortal, for that is all the help you'll ever get. I know."

And, so saying, he walked away and the Marids barred and bolted the door behind him.

"Zongri," said Jan, going to the place where the queen had stood, "coming here—for me!" And a cold chill of horror went up and down his spine. But suddenly he straightened and marched back to the bed where he tossed off two drinks neat.

He threw the empty bottle aside and ripped off the white silk robe. Placing the ring upon his wrist—so large it was—he addressed himself to the task of getting on boots and pants and shirt.

"Zongri will take care of me in time. But before that, by Allah and Bal and Confucius, I've still a dancing girl to see!" And who knew, he thought, hauling on a boot, but what this same dancing girl, who might be Alice Hall, would prove his salvation at least in the other world?

TWELVE

He stood squarely before the door and Jan took a deep breath as though for a plunge into cold water and Tiger fingered the great Seal upon his wrist and chuckled. The ring had struck Zongri's fetters from him and now, now he would investigate its efficacy on other types of locks.

"By the Seal of Sulayman! Open wide!"

Jan almost leaped out of his wits at the resulting crash, so certain was he that it would be heard by every jinni in the palace. On the instant of command every bar, inside and out, leaped upward from its bracket and fell down with a clang. The great lock was rent as though a bolt of lightning had struck it. The portal smashed back against the wall and Jan stood facing three astounded Marids.

But he was braced to go, and they were too startled to properly receive him until he was almost upon them. And then their swords sang from the scabbards and the first lunged with his pike.

Tiger took a step sideways and the pike passed him by. He ducked and a saber clanged into steel just over his head. He skipped back away from the slash of the third and instantly drove into him like a battering-ram.

They left the top step like an explosion, the Marid's scarlet cloak wrapping them all about and billowing as they fell down the flight.

Tiger, like his name, came up standing at the bottom—standing on the chest of a very battered Marid.

Scooping up the guard's saber and pistols and hurling back jeers at the howling pair who charged down from the top, he raced to the next flight and took it in three jumps. He was in a corridor and for a moment he had to think out the palace's plan. Then, knowing that it was inevitable to avoid going through most of it, and with the yells of the Marids banging his ear-drums, he again raced forward and down another flight.

Around the next landing he heard voices but so great was his speed that he could not check himself. Like a catapulted stone he shot toward five officers who instantly faced about, recognized him and snatched at their swords.

Jan knocked them sprawling in five directions and though a little stunned himself, did not consider it necessary to pause and help any of them up. He soared like an eagle down the next flight, hope burning in him that he could find a way around the great audience chamber. But so great was his speed, with proportionately little time for scouting, that before he could check himself he was thirty feet into the enormous hall and charging straight at the throne.

Ramus had given irate instructions for the city's defense, and when she thought she beheld a rambunctious page she started to roar out at him.

The floor was so slippery that it was almost like skating. Jan curved away and though still two hundred feet from the throne, the queen cried, "*Tiger!*"

He was already diving toward the immense black doors, estimating the guard across it. So far they were faced the other way, and if they would only stay so, he had a chance of getting through them.

"*Tiger!*" roared Ramus and when again he disregarded her she shouted, "Take him! Captain of the guard, *stop that man!*"

As one, the cordon before the doors whirled around, pikes up. It was like a picket fence leaning over and

every point glittered hungrily to receive him. He could not stop because of his speed and the floor. And though—who knows?—Ramus might have had it otherwise, the order stood and the instinct of the pike soldier is to spear whatever he sees.

"Tiger, you fool! You'll be killed!" . .

But he was even then on the pikes—or rather, *almost* on them, there being quite a difference. For Tiger, with all a sailor's agility, slashed sideways with his saber, engaging two pikes at once and feinting them aside, to plunge instantly through the gap. The Marids saw steel flash before their faces and, astounded by the maneuver, ducked back. And by the time they had recovered to again level their weighty weapons for the kill, Tiger was fifty feet away from them and multiplying the distance with alacrity.

Ahead was yet another cordon, that which guarded the outside doors. And these, hearing the clash of steel on steel, were alert and waiting, soon astonished to find that a human being was racing out of the palace toward them. These men had ample warning and Tiger saw in the instant that they could not miss stopping him.

To his right and left were other great doors, leading into the depths of the palace again. He did not think twice. He roared: "By the Seal of Sulayman! Open wide!"

The right-hand door crashed open, its lock so much iron junk. Beyond a large room yawned. But already the guards were advancing from the front entrance and Tiger waited not at all but plunged in.

He was over the threshold before he saw that he had come to the last place in Tarbuton that he wanted to be—the office of Ramus' chief of staff!

The soldiers in the place stiffened in their chairs and along the wall to see a sailor dash in without any more ceremony than a bloodthirsty flourish of a saber. Instantly they perceived that an assassination was in order.

The general fired point-blank with the pistol he always kept on his desk. But the ball buried itself a good foot above Tiger's damp head. Steel flashed as men made for him.

Tiger had no time to think about it. Battle was battle to him. But Jan cried out: "By the Seal of Sulayman! Down with the wall!"

With a thunder of cracking stone, the front of the room fell outward, obscuring everything in a white cloud of mortar. The flash and roar which had followed the order and the sunlight which abruptly poured in upon them held the soldiers for a terrified instant.

Jan leaped through the fog in the opening and clutched at a vine which grew down the building's face. Earth smote the soles of his boots and he raced off on the rebound, diving into the protection of shrubbery and running bent over while branches sought to flog him.

The uproar he left behind him was spreading like the waves of a rock dropped into a pool. He saw an outpost dashing in toward the palace and ducked low, halting for an instant. The scarlet cloaks streamed by and an instant later he leaped into their dust and sped toward their unprotected section. The sentry boxes fled by on his right, and he dashed through the deep dust of a roar to gain the less pretentious and more welcome rank of stores which faced the square.

Citizenry gaped at him. A Marid in green instantly suspected the worst and scudded in pursuit, his long green cape pouring after him and the whistle in his mouth trilling hysterically.

Jan sprang into an alleyway and pressed himself against the wall. The policeman rounded the turn an instant later. Tiger stuck out a foot and the officer went down with two hundred pounds of sailor to pin him to earth and still the whistle. Tiger trussed the Marid with the green cape and then, not waiting to see if the alarm had been answered, surveyed the scene about him and decided upon a drain pipe which led to a two-story building above.

Like the sailor he was, he dug in his toes and hand over hand rocketed up the sheer face. He flung himself over the parapet at the top and looked down. Two policemen had answered the call promptly, but they were just now arriving beside their squirming, swearing brother at law and their immediate attention was for him and not a possible quarry.

Jan drew back his head. Before him, side by side, stretched a long avenue of roofs, inviting him to try his broadjumping proclivities. He took the dare but he traveled at a slightly slower pace, for he was feeling his exertions a little.

An hour later, having startled three separate sunbathing parties out of their respective wits but without having met with any further misadventure, he came to the base of the hill toward which he had stubbornly worked. He let himself to earth and sought a clump of trees and there, sprawled at length, he got his breath and gazed admiringly at the architecture of his goal. Before very long, his admiration turned to something very near dismay. The priests who had caused this place to be constructed had kept a watchful eye upon their own security.

The great, varicolored cube which, like the head of some monster, swallowed and disgorged thousands of jinn, was high and aloof upon its hill. And though grass grew upon those precipitous slopes it definitely ended the landscaping. This place was a fort! And the canny high lords of it gave no intruder a single tree for cover. It was the crowning insult to see priest sentries on a parapet which ran the circuit of the roof. Tiger fumed. One had to ascend those steps or wait for night, and he was not fatuous enough to suppose that he could pass his brawny humanity for an Ifrit.

Night, he decided disconsolately, it would have to be.

Though he well apprehended the danger of entering the town again, he was aware of thirst and hunger and suddenly bethought himself of a certain deep dive where the proprietor was indebted to him through said proprietor's undue faith in dice. Jan smiled as he very vividly remembered a night when Tiger had won the place, tables, hostesses and kegs and had magnanimously loaned it all back forever. It was weird to recollect such a thing because Jan had never experienced it himself, just as Tiger couldn't have told one end of an astrolabe from another. But now Tiger could work an astrolabe and, no doubt, Jan could shoot dice with maddening precision.

By alleyways in which his feet were trained, he flitted through the dusky shadows and came, at last, to the rear entrance of the dive. Cautiously he edged in and peered at the occupants of the taproom.

Several human beings, persons who were very much in keeping with the dingy furtiveness of the place, sat at the scarred tables along the wall, drinking questionable beverages. As long as they were human, Tiger knew he had nothing to fear from them and so boldly entered, marching up to the bar and casually greeting the keeper.

He was a man of rotund build, placid and usually cheerful, and because of those attributes and his obvious docility, he was allowed to operate his tavern, though it was a favor rarely accorded humans.

His mild little eyes turned to Tiger, started to move away and then came back with a crack and pop. "Good God! *You!*"

"And what's the matter with that?" said Tiger.

"Listen," said the proprietor in an excited whisper, "you've got to get out of here. They know you come here! The alarm is out for you and not ten seconds ago there was a squad of Marids here looking for you!"

"Then they won't be back very soon. Lazy fellows, Marids. Would you mind digging into the larder and setting forth fare fit for a gentleman? I'm famished!"

The tavern keeper eyed him wonderingly. "You ain't

scared. I know you wouldn't be scared. But you ought to have pity on me. Just think what'll they do if they find you here! Geez, Tiger, I don't know what you done, but the patrol was the queen's Desert Troopers and they looked upset as hell."

"The queen objects to my leaving her tea party. If they come back I'll swear you didn't recognize me. How is that?"

The man was very doubtful but he was not able to withstand Tiger. He stuck his head through a square hole and spoke to his wife in the kitchen. Then he looked at Tiger again and dabbed at his forehead with his apron.

"Hot, ain't it?" he said weakly.

"Can't say as I've noticed," said Tiger with a grin.

The proprietor puttered with glasses, and his hands shook so that he almost dropped three in a batch. He gave it up. "Look, Tiger. Like a good guy, would you go over to that table agin' the wall and make yourself as small as possible?"

Tiger shrugged. "It's all the same as long as the food is good and there's lots of it." He wandered to the designated spot and was about to seat himself. Suddenly he started.

At the table next to his were two men he was certain he knew, and yet for the life of him he could not place them. One was hook-nosed and spidery-handed and possessed two liabilities in the form of evil, bloodshot eyes. The other was obese and as slick as though he had been freshly lubricated—though with somewhat rancid oil. They were quite obviously of a certain class of slaves whose masters specialized in the lower orders of crime and had a kicked-cur look about them which filled a beholder with disgust.

Tiger lowered himself slowly into his chair. He was very puzzled. He usually remembered faces very easily and the names as well. Though he told himself that he would not ordinarily notice such vermin and that he had seen them here on other occasions, he was not at all convinced. Who, he demanded of himself, were they?

Presently the proprietor came with a ham and a chicken and three bottles of different wines. His cargo sounded like castanets and he almost missed the table with it, so intent was he upon the door. Hurriedly he made a second trip for bread and then withdrew to morosely seat himself at the end of his bar and keep an eye upon the place from which he was certain doom would soon enter in the form of the queen's Desert Troopers.

Tiger ate slowly, pondering his problem and somewhat annoyed that he would bother to dwell upon two such scurvy beings. There was a certain familiarity about them which was incongruous, and then Jan's fund of knowledge took a hand.

"I'm changed," Jan whispered. "Why couldn't it be possible for these two to be known to me in the other world?"

And, with that as a starting point, he carefully surveyed their features until he was as exasperated as though he had a word on the end of his tongue and couldn't say it.

At last the two gentlemen in question, being two to Jan's one, took exception to his scrutiny. They muttered about it in low tones and evidently decided that it wasn't to be tolerated. The one with the bloodshot eyes came ominously to his feet and stalked over to Jan's table.

"If you got something to spill, out with it, pal."

The obese member of the duet waddled over to back his partner up. Jan looked from one to the other of them and they mistook his attitude for apology.

"All right," said the fat one. "But don't git so nosy, see?"

And they would have walked back had not a bolt of lightning struck in the center of Jan's brain. "Wait a minute. I know you fellows."

"Yeah, well, we don't know you and don't want to, neither. So if—"

"You," said Jan, seeing the almost indefinable line of features at last and pointing to the nervous one, "are Nathaniel Green!"

"Huh?" said the indicated one.

"And you," said Jan in sudden excitement, "are Shannon! That's it! That's it! I could feel it! Look, sit down. I've got a matter to talk over with you."

"He's cockroachy," said the indicated Green.

"Look, buddy," said the greasy caricature of Shannon, "we're minding our own business and if you want to pick daisies from the under side, you'll forget to mind your own."

But Jan was laughing, looking from one to the other of them. "Green! Poor old Nathaniel Green. Where's your watch? And you! Shannon! A tub of lard with a coating of dirt and as surly as a kicked pariah!" His laugh grew louder.

The pair were uneasy on more than one count. They were quite aware of the pistols in Tiger's belt and of the size of Tiger's shoulders and were somewhat intimidated by the correct language springing from a sailor's mouth. It looked like a magic spy trap to them and they weren't having any. They shuffled, growling, back to their table, got their hats, haggled over the reckoning and left.

"Who are those men?" asked Jan when the keeper came over to find out the cause of the argument.

"Them? Gutter pickin's. Dauda's jackals. They eat his leavin's. What's the idea gettin' me in trouble with a guy like Dauda? Ain't you got no sense, Tiger? You come back here with the troopers on your trail, talkin' like a swell and lookin'—well, lookin' different. I wouldn'a' knowed you at first. But listen, Tiger, will you finish up and get out of here? You know you're welcome to anything I got, but they'll be comin' back pretty soon and it's as much as my life is worth. After all, the queen's Desert Troopers don't go pokin' around unless a man's assassinated a duke or something."

"All right. To save your nerves I'll finish and go," said Tiger. "Besides, I don't think much of your trade, anyway. They stink."

Dusk found him again at the foot of the temple hill. The enormous cube stood out against angry clouds and from every entrance there streamed the light of flaming braziers. Torches flanked the avenue of steps, and their fitful flare fell weirdly upon the throng of jinn. Evidently some great rite was to be held, for all the crowd marched upward and none marched down, and it was plain from the fanfare of flashing jewels that the worshipers were dressed for some state occasion. Perhaps, thought Jan, the word has gone about that Zongri comes with a fleet from the Barbossis. But whatever it was, his chances of entering that place undiscovered were very remote indeed.

He was almost on the verge of turning back when there again came to him the vision of the dancing girl upon the steps and, simultaneously, the memory of the girl who had shown him the only kindness he had ever received. She was there, a dancing slave to the jinn, and who knew but what the morrow would find him dead in this world and, consequently, the other as well. Certainly he owed it to her to try, if he could, to free her and give her into the keeping of one who would repay favor with favor—Admiral Tyronin, whose influence was great enough to protect her and who, even in the event of defeat, would very probably be suffered to retire to his island estate on parole. High officers, remembered Tiger, seldom suffered greatly in these wars.

No, he could not leave her there to be ultimately thieved by some persuasive jinn—as was the fate of these dancing girls. And besides, every atom of him demanded to confront her and speak to her, for it grew upon him that she alone might save him in his own world.

Tiger strode forward, skirting the mound until he came to the rear. As on a cliff the temple blazed above him, Marids in silhouette upon the walls. He loosened his saber in its sheath and looked to the priming of his pistols and then began the ascent.

Of all mortals, only dancing girls had come here in the history of the place, except those few who had dared it to end upon a pike at the foot of the steps, grinning at awed beholders. There was treasure in this place to tempt even honest men and in the town it was sometimes said of a thief that he was bold enough to "scale the heights of Rani."

Tiger, scaling the heights, was not thinking about being bold but only of discovering an entrance and making his way through the place to the quarters of the dancers. The long grass caught at his boots and strove to hold him back, but he made it pay by grasping handfuls of it and so hoisting himself upward. It was no great trick to ascend the slope, but Tiger had been giving his attention to the ground and did not see the next barrier until he had almost fallen into it. The dark hole gaped and he held hard to the edge, one foot already into it. Hastily he drew back, eyeing the trap in the flare of the torches above. Here, dug so as to be unseen from the plain below, was a moat about thirty feet wide and as deep. But no water was here, only a hiss and rattle as things moved on the floor.

"Snakes!" said Tiger, feeling the hair rise on the back of his neck. He took a hitch on his nerve and felt with his foot over the edge. But the drop was sheer and the slimy things at the bottom rustled as they moved to the foot of the drop, waiting.

He cursed impatiently at such jinn hellishness. But he wasted very little time mourning about it. He had only one recourse—to ascend by the stairs through the main entrance!

He made the decision and put it into action at once, striding along the outer edge of the moat, watchful for other traps but well informed by the lights above.

Shortly he had come again to the front of the building and, dropping on his face, crept toward the great balustrades, toward stronger light and toward guards.

Marids were posted at the end of every wide step, their steel helmets as bright as their single eyes and their pikes bearing streamers which did not in the least impair their usefulness. But so stately was their bearing and so bright the torches in their eyes that Jan was able to come within touching distance of one's back without being seen. He lay in the protection of the balustrade's shadow and pondered his next move. More and more, as obstacles arose, he determined to put his plan into action, and now he was certain that his salvation, at least on earth, depended upon his reaching Alice Hall in this world.

He was very sorely tempted to steal the sentry's cloak, but he well knew the folly of trying to pass off his brawn for a Marid's stumpy ugliness. So he began to work himself up toward the temple by keeping in the shadow of the steps where the jinn thronged not ten feet away. He wondered a little just what method of killing they would use if they caught him; regardless of how the queen might want him treated, the priests of Rani would do—as they rightfully did—whatever they pleased. As excaptive of the throne, sought by troopers, perhaps a lash would be the most he merited. But he well knew that if he invaded Rani, the long arm of that goddess would find him in whatever state or abode he sought refuge. But he wasn't caught yet.

Again he almost tripped into the moat and was angered to find that it butted against this pavement's edge. Had he gone to all this trouble only to be balked by the same barrier? He raised his head a little and stared at the crowd whose brilliant robes almost brushed his face. He again eyed the moat. And then,

bethinking himself of the urgency of his mission, gripped the edge of the pavement and swung himself over the darkly tenanted space.

He swung himself along, holding to the slippery edge of the steps, trusting that his hands would escape being seen. The torches were bright and his luck was in at the moment so he came to safety on the other side. Again he examined the ground about him. The temple's foundation was about eight feet high and on it stood columns whose backs were against the stone walls. He sprang up to the ledge. Somewhere there must be a postern. Above him on the roof, guards paced mechanically back and forth like great black dolls. To his left spread the colorful panorama of the steps and behind him, far below, sparkled the lights of harbor and city.

His questing fingers examined the wall ahead of him and then, with relief, they touched the cold iron of a small door. It was locked, but that worried him not at all.

"By the Seal of Sulayman," he whispered, "open wide."

THIRTEEN

Softly the door swung inward as though pulled by an unseen hand. Jan slipped through the opening and silently closed the portal. He was in a long hall, momentarily deserted. Through the archways which flanked it he could see the limitless expanse of the temple's main room where torches flared smokily and set gigantic shadows to chasing each other along the walls and ceiling.

At the far end was a gargantuan idol, all of gold and silver and ivory, gleaming with precious stones. The hands rested upon the hilt of a sword some fifty feet long and the feet were spread apart in an attitude of battle. This was Rani, Rani goddess of the jinn, terrible of eye, lovely of form, lustful and mystic, beauteous and murderous. Other humans—and few they had been—had paid for such a sight with their lives.

Jan tore his eyes away from the terrifying figure and cast about him for further ways. But he dared go neither up nor down this hall, for at each end he could see temple guards and passing crowds. And certainly he could not walk forward into the place of worship. Sailorlike he looked aloft and took heart. The wall was built in gradually narrowing stones and each one offered a ledge, four feet above the last. And the columns which supported the roof were interconnected by beams.

He heard someone close a door near at hand and the mutter of voices approaching. He lost no time swinging up and leaping from ledge to ledge. A moment later he looked down upon the horned heads of priests. They paused, talking together, before they entered the great chamber.

"Then it is settled," said the oldest of the lot, one dressed all in yellow silk. "He cannot injure us, for he is one of the believers and so also are his very warriors. What, then, say you to the prophecy of defeat for Ramus?"

They held up their clawed right hands in the Ifrit gesture of the affirmative.

"It is time," said another, "that we were accorded greater freedom here. A plague on Ramus. Let the prophecy ring loud enough to take the hearts out of the officers here. He will repay it handsomely with greater freedom."

"Very well," said the old one. "Let the rites begin."

They moved out of the shadows, and while some of them went furtively down through a trap in the floor, the others, including the ancient one, walked boldly out into the chamber itself.

Jan pondered their words. Certainly, by "he" could they mean Zongri? And Tiger, of a sudden, remembered vague rumors of dissatisfaction among the priesthood for Ramus' refusal to take part in their rites and her placing such great reliance upon the soothsayer Zeno and his stars. Zeno had broken the monopoly of Rani on prophecy when the queen had elevated him to his high place.

Now that the hall below was deserted, Jan dropped swiftly down to it again with a new idea. He opened the trap in the floor, found a steep stairway leading through gloom. He closed the trap over him and made his way along a tunnel which seemed to lead for miles beneath the earth. Wiping cobwebs from his face and pausing constantly to listen and look for possible guards, he finally reached the end of it. Here was another stairway, going up.

Somewhere far off he heard a hundred mighty

horns bellow hoarsely for silence. And as he mounted, the single voice of a speaker came to him with increasing distinctness. Then he came to a parting of the stairs. One continued up but the other led off on the level. Jan chose the ascent rather than run a chance of losing himself in a labyrinth.

By the number of steps he knew that he was well above the floor of the great chamber and that he must now be within one of the walls. Again the way became level and he found that he had entered upon an observation gallery.

He was not much amazed, being well versed in such abstruse subjects as ordinary necromancy, to find that sets of eyeholes were bored through the stone so as to match with the eyes of figures with which the chamber was decorated. He wondered that the jinn permitted such an obvious trick, and his opinion of their wits fell accordingly.

The chamber was spread out before him in all its shadowy splendor. Full ten thousand jinn, resplendent in sparkling jewels and shimmering silk, stood upon the gradually raised floor. They faced Rani but between them and the idol intervened a semi-circle where a mass of priests were now undergoing some sort of ritual. Their bowed heads were all inclined toward Rani and over them rolled the sepulchral tones of the temple master, he who had been in the hall near Jan.

What he was saying Jan neither knew nor cared. All his attention was concentrated upon the ringing rank of temple dancers who were intermingled with Marids in rite regalia. One by one he studied the girls, but in those hundreds and at this height above them, he found it very difficult to find Alice Hall. His spine tingled as he thought of her there, a part of that savage splendor, hypnotized by the intoning music which now began to flow from an unseen recess in the chamber. At this signal the girls stood up, throwing back their white capes and stepping ahead of the

Marids, their diamond-decked bodies rose in the guttering torchlight.

Suddenly he found her. She was a pace or two ahead of all the rest and seemed to be a key to their movements. He hardly knew what the others did, though he was conscious of their forming geometric patterns in slow, easy grace to the increasing tempo of the horns and drums.

With difficulty he bethought himself of Rani and turned his attention to the idol. The enormous figure was supported by heavy chains so placed as to be invisble from the front. And so it was not with as great a shock as the others below that he saw the goddess begin to move slowly from side to side.

Puerile, he thought to himself. Probably the thing was hinged like a marionette and, without doubt, it had speaking tubes connected with it so that priests could simulate its voice.

The music became faster, louder, and he found that he had been unconsciously beating to it. The wild strains, guttural and hoarse, brought the hot blood pulsing to his face, and it was with difficulty that he tore his eyes away from the idol.

He knew quite well what he intended to do just as he completely understood the horrible consequences which might follow. But Tiger was bold and Jan was cunning, and in a moment he strode down the runway, searching for yet another passageway which might admit him to the chamber itself when the occasion came. But his only chance lay in the one branch he had found and now he paced down it, watching ahead of each turn, certain that he would run into priests.

Finally he found another branch, but this one led straight up, and that he did not need. Ahead he saw two spots of light and came up against a short ladder. By mounting it he again discovered that he could see out and that, also, he could get out when that occasion came.

It did not take him long to find that he was inside

the idol's base, for, by looking straight up he could see the gigantic wings which sprouted stiffly from the goddess's shoulders and swooped earthward toward him.

He was slightly puzzled to see that the goddess had taken her hand from the sword and now held her arms out straight above the heads of the dancers. From this angle the goddess had a staring look which was awful to see.

The dancers swayed and dipped and the music quickened. Soon they were in a semicircle, spinning like tops, their hair flying out from their heads and their supple bodies weaving. With a crash the music stopped. In the deep stillness the dancers fled back until they were again in their original places. Throwing themselves down in an attitude of supplication, they waited.

The priests spread away, leaving only their ancient blackguard of a master. The venerable one spread out his hands to the goddess. Somewhere a drum beat hysterically for an instant and then was still. From his cassock the master took a long, shining whip and let it curl like a snake along the pavement. Again the drums shattered the stillness and deepened it by their ceasing. The master's whip cracked like a musket.

"Rani!" cried the ancient one. "Rani! By the symbol of this whip with which we hold you, we demand that you answer!"

The goddess was not swinging now. The feet moved until they were together. The head, fully a dozen yards in diameter, bent so that the glowing eyes stared down at the master.

"Rani! Behold! We have offered you music and dancing. We offer you worship! Answer and answer well!"

Again the whip cracked and Rani moved a trifle while a flutter of awe ran back through the crowd.

Jan thought to himself that the jinn were a witless lot to be fooled by a hundred-and-fifty-foot marionette.

"Who," cried the master, "shall be the victor in tomorrow's battle? Zongri, or Ramus the Magnificent?"

A deep, unintelligible rumble came from the goddess.

And then, from the sides of the hall, on two platforms near to Rani's head, the priests Jan had seen before took station. In their hands they held long poles which had glowing coals on their ends. With these they thrust at the goddess's shoulder.

A tremor shot through the idol which Jan thought very well done. Again the master cried out.

"Rani, who shall be the victor? *Answer!*"

A snarl of pain and rage followed. The stare in those glassy eyes changed to a waking expression of wrath. Rani moved and the chains rattled savagely.

"*Answer!*" howled the master.

A flood of strange words poured from the moving lips, to hurl across the chamber and rebound like a cannonade.

"Be still!" cried the master. He whirled about. "Rani has spoken! Woe to Tarbuton. The fate of the battle will fall upon the banners of Zongri—and Ramus will be vanquished forever!"

A gasp ran through the chamber, a sound which expressed shock and growing terror.

Again the goddess spoke, unbidden, in those rolling accents. But the men on the platform beside her head stabbed out with the coals and Rani was still.

"Now," thought Jan, "while their wits are paralyzed, I'll show them how their goddess lies—in fragments at their feet!"

He raised the ring and cried: "By the Seal of Sulayman! Part the chains!"

Mortar flew from the walls in great, angry puffs. Iron clanked in falling and then crashed resoundingly to the floor. The ancient one whirled and stared with disbelief at the monstrous figure which teetered forward toward him.

Jan ducked, waiting for the concussion of the fall. It

came before he expected it—so violently that the stone cracked wide before him and the whole temple rocked!

He heard a scream of terror from the jinn and then the rush of twenty thousand feet seeking exit through the dust-choked gloom.

Tiger sprang out of his observation post and raced across the floor. Because the dancing girls were farthest from the entrance, they huddled against the jam, staring with terrified eyes at the fallen goddess, half of them probably convinced of its former power.

Tiger waded through broken granite and chips of gold. Under his feet rolled the diamonds which had bedecked the headdress. He had eyes only for one jewel, the dancing girl nearest to him. So stunned was she that she remarked not at all that it was a human being who came racing out of that fog of dust. Her lovely eyes were round with horror and did not even turn to him when he scooped her up into his arms.

The priests were as mad as the rest to get away from there, failing to understand that nothing else could happen. The death of their master had unnerved them and two rushed by Tiger within a foot without paying the slightest attention to him. Tiger disliked being ignored. When the largest priest struck the jam, Tiger snatched him by the shoulder, tearing away the flowing yellow cloak which had covered him from crown to toe. The Ifrit scarcely noticed the loss.

Throwing the color of protection about them, Jan bore the girl through the packed masses, bullying a way out of the entrance and down the long stairs. Unnoticed, he reached the avenue at the bottom and dodged into a side street as soon as one presented itself. The weight of the dancing girl was slight and impeded him but little.

Already terror was beginning to spread through the city and, far off, bells were ringing and horns blowing. Jan cared nothing about them. By alley and dark thoroughfare he sped swiftly to the waterfront, hardly pausing at all to leap down off a dock into a small fishing smack.

The fisherman leaped up from his dozing on a pile of nets and his two sailors came up standing a moment later. They were still asleep so far as their wits went, for Tiger had only to let the dock lights glitter on the saber and cry, "To the *Morin*, flagship of Admiral Tyronin!"

The sailors mechanically cast off, seeing in Tiger an espionage officer or some other in whom they would not dare take any great interest. The lateen sail dropped from its yard and filled and in the fresh night wind they scudded between anchored vessels whose lights made yellow sea serpents upon the water.

The girl had been staring at Tiger for some time and, seeing him smile at her, she spoke. "Who . . . who are you?"

"Tiger."

"*You are Tiger?*"

"Does notoriety reach even to a jinn temple?"

"I have heard naval officers ask a blessing for you. But–how is it that you entered the temple? That is death to a human!"

"For once it wasn't. Not yet, anyway."

"But why–" she hesitated in sudden fear. "Why have you taken me away?"

"Did you like that place?"

"Oh! No, no! I am glad to be stolen. But–"

"You have no need to be afraid." It seemed so strange to see Alice Hall here and yet not to be known to her. "You have never seen me before?"

"Why . . . of course not. I have seen no human being other than my dancers since I was a child."

"Have you ever heard the name, Alice Hall?"

She repeated it slowly after him, a puzzled look upon her face. "Al . . . ice. Alice Hall. I seem to have heard it somewhere before."

"Of course you have. You *are* Alice Hall."

"I?" she shook her head. "But no, I have no name but Wanna. You are making fun of me."

"No indeed."

"You are a very strange fellow. Why did you come to the temple?"

"To get you."

"Me?"

"I saw you once before—here. In a telescope."

She looked unwinkingly at him and drew the yellow cloak more tightly about her against the cold wind. She ventured a smile and clutched at his hand as he turned to watch the side of the flagship come up to them.

The fishermen brailed their sail and the boat drifted in to the landing stage. Jan took a hoop out of his ear and handed it to the captain who stared at it in amazement, changing his opinion about espionage instantly.

Tiger took up the girl again and trotted up the ladder to the deck where a jinn officer stood with threatening mien.

"I wish to be taken to Admiral Tyronin immediately," said Tiger.

The officer scowled.

"My name is Tiger."

It was as though he had stuck a pin in the lieutenant. The Ifrit whirled to his lounging guard. "Take this man into custody immediately."

"I demand to see the admiral!" cried Jan.

A voice from the quarterdeck of the seventy-four smote them. "What is this?" And boots thumped on a ladder and over the planks and so into the light of the guard lantern.

With relief Jan recognized Commander Hakon who had stopped him before the palace.

"Tiger!" cried the commander. "Good God, man, what are you doing here? Get back ashore. Lieutenant, call that boat—"

"I'm to see Admiral Tyronin," said Tiger. "And see him I shall."

"But what is this you have here?" Hakon saw the yellow robe. "The cloak of . . . of a priest!" Then he saw the girl's flashing jewels. "And . . . and a temple dancer! Tiger, have you gone mad? Was it you who caused that commotion up at the temple which we have been hearing and watching for half an hour?"

"That's neither here nor there," said Tiger. "I asked a favor."

"On your head be it," said the commander. "His lordship is just about out of his head, what with expecting to meet forty ships with four and then all that uproar over on the beach. What was it about?"

"Rani fell over on her face," said Jan.

"What?"

"Because she lied," said the dancing girl swiftly. "She said that Zongri would win and a greater god smote her."

Hakon blanched.

"The admiral," reminded Tiger.

"Well, remember that you asked for it," said Hakon dispiritedly. He led the way aft and to the quarterdeck. They descended a short ladder and found themselves in the admiral's quarters. The door of the inner room was open and Tiger could see the ugly and now worried Tyronin bent over a chart, pencil poised. The light of the lanthorn increased the lines of his hairy face.

"Your lordship," said Hakon, bowing slightly.

"Yes? Yes, what is it now?"

"You perhaps recall a sailor called Tiger who once brought us the line which pulled us off the beach on the Isle of Fire when—"

"Tiger? Yes, what about him now?" Tyronin saw the man and stood up. The group moved into the room and his lordship started at both yellow cloak and dancing girl. "What's this?" he thundered.

"Sir," said Tiger, "tomorrow you are to meet Zongri

in battle. I am the chief cause of his coming attack and for that reason I–"

"Bah! I only know that you are trying to play upon my generosity and make trouble for me with the queen. Did you know that the town is being combed for you? No, I suppose not! Did you know that you are to be arrested on sight? Oh no, of course not! You thought I would blind myself to my duty to her majesty and take you in like some stray cur! You come with a Rani dancing girl with probably the blood of a priest upon your hands as well as his cloak and expect me–God! *Guard!*"

"Wait," pleaded Tiger. "I–"

"*Silence!* Guard, place this man under arrest. Put the dancing girl in Lurgo's cabin and make certain she does not escape. This man is Tiger. You may have heard of him. He is not to be trusted for an instant. You are to make certain that a sentry with a primed pistol stands outside his cell with the muzzle of that weapon trained upon him whether he is waking or sleeping. There!" He faced Tiger. "At midnight we weigh anchor to meet Zongri's fleet. It is too late to put you ashore now. But if fortune favors us you'll be surrendered to the queen on our return."

The sentry took Tiger's pistols and saber and at pistol point escorted him back to the deck. Tiger was conscious of the girl's despairing eyes upon his back– and conscious, too, of the short-lived gratitude of man.

FOURTEEN

Jan awoke to the uneasy realization that elsewhere he was asleep with a cocked pistol pointing at him and as the body, alive but without vital force, might roll and turn, he hoped that Tiger would offer no offense.

He swung his feet down to the concrete floor and found that Diver had been restored to him. But Diver was still snoring and Jan wondered where Diver was and what Diver was doing. Someday he would find out, perhaps, though he was not very interested. And the counterfeiters—where were they and what were they doing while their earth bodies snored so resoundingly? Not, of course, that it mattered much.

He sighed deeply and stuffed the pipe Alice had brought him and got it going. Thoughtfully he reviewed Tiger's deeds and misdeeds. He was almost dispassionate about it—for a little while. With the theft of the dancing girl, Tiger had stamped his death warrant. While nobody could prove that he had had any connection with the destruction of Rani, merely the touching of a sacred member of that temple would doom him. And the queen? What would she say when she found how he had duped her about that Seal?

Soon he began to sweat. Certain he was that that night he would sleep himself into death. Tyronin's foolhardy resistance to Zongri's great fleet would probably doom the ship. If, somehow, it didn't, Zongri would find him. Whether Ramus or Zongri held forth for victory, Tiger's puckish pranks were over. As it was early he lay back upon his bunk and tried to dispose himself for further slumber. But he was too nervous for that and thought he interspersed visions of a pointed cocked pistol framed in a door with a pair of cockroaches climbing sturdily being half in and half out of each world, he found no rest in either.

He was almost glad when the jail began to stir about but he was far too worried to enjoy his food. He listened to Diver's gibes and heard them not at all. And as the morning progressed he found he could not sit still but must walk up and down by the bars.

Finally, at eleven, they came for him, Shannon and a guard. Shannon's false heartiness sought to cheer him up.

"Now you just do what I tell you, Jan, and this'll all be O.K. We'll let you tell your story just as it happened, and then I'll throw what weight I can behind it and pretty soon we'll have you out of here slick as grease."

Jan didn't answer and Shannon kept it up until they came to an antechamber to the judge's office where a thin, skeleton-faced fellow sat thumping the table with his pince-nez.

"This's Doc Harrington," said Shannon. "This's Jan Palmer, doc."

"Ah," said Harrington, looking professionally at Jan. "Let us get down to business." He put forth pencil and paper and invited Jan to sit and write the answers to certain questions and, when that was done, to put down the first word which came into his mind after another word was given. That too was over shortly.

The psychiatrist examined the result and his brows went up, up, up until they almost vanished in his sparse hair. He pursed his lips and pulled his beard. He adjusted his pince-nez and took them off. He scowled at Jan and then read the paper once more.

"O.K.?" said Shannon.

"Ah . . . yes. Splendid."

"Then, let's go."

They entered the judge's office where batteries of

legal books stood ready to fire opinions on any sort of case imaginable and where nervous feet had worn out the rug by the desk.

The judge was a well-fed, rather dull person who carried his dignity of office very easily—never having been bothered with any original thoughts and so injure it.

"Sit down," said the judge.

Jan sat down and looked around him. Aunt Ethel was there, dabbing at her eyes—which were quite dry—and muttering, "Oh, the poor boy, the poor boy."

Thompson sat against the other wall, gnawing on a bowler. Nathaniel Green paced back and forth, looking at his watch and complaining about the delay.

For an instant Jan was frightened, and then became flooded with relief when he saw Alice Hall sitting at a small desk ready to take down the proceedings for Green's edification. She looked wonderingly at Jan but beyond that made no sign.

"Now, let's get down to it," said the judge. "In brief, young man, sketch your story of how Professor Frobish came to be murdered. We're all your friends here so you need have no fear."

Jan looked them over and experienced a desire to laugh in the judge's face. With the exception of Alice there wasn't a person in the room who had the least desire to find him innocent. Indeed, Aunt Ethel and Thompson, Shannon and, last but not least, Green, stood to profit enormously by his bad luck.

"Just say I'm crazy and have done with it," said Jan truculently. "No matter what I say, that will be the verdict."

"Why, my poor boy," whimpered Aunt Ethel, "you're among your own—"

"I'd rather be in a hyena's den," said Jan. He noted how they all started at his tone. "Well, with nothing to gain or lose, I may as well give you the truth." And, so saying, he very briefly sketched the facts of the case.

When he had done with his terse statements, the psychiatrist unobtrusively placed his penciled findings upon the judge's desk and the judge bent over it for some time. Then he sat back, making a steeple out of his fingers and nodding. Just when everyone thought he had gone to sleep, he rang for his clerk and sent out for a form. When he came, he filled in a few blanks and then turned to Green.

"You will have to sign this. You and the two others."

Shannon almost leaped for the pen when Green was done. And Thompson and Aunt Ethel had quite a lively race for it. But Aunt Ethel won and signed her name with vague murmurs about what a terrible shame it was and how insanity would have to run in the Palmer family that way. She didn't see how she could ever live it down.

The formalities over, the judge reached toward a buzzer.

"Wait a minute," said Jan, getting up.

The judge sat back and then again, more hurriedly this time, bent a finger toward the button.

"If this is justice," said Jan, "I'm going to work for the anarchists. You've heard nothing sufficient to convince you that my story is or is not true. These people," and he took them in with the wave of his hand, "are only too anxious to have me put away."

There were murmurs which showed that the company demurred heartily.

"You have not even called," said Jan, "for exhibit A."

"Ex-exhibit A?" said the judge. "But my dear fellow, calm yourself. This is all very irregular—"

"There is the matter of looking at the copper jar," said Jan.

"But I see no necessity—" began Green impatiently.

"You mean there really is a copper jar?" said the judge.

"Indeed there is," said Jan. "How about it, Alice?"

"Why, certainly there is," she said swiftly, though to tell the truth she had never so much as noticed it in all her visits there.

"And an examination of that jar," said Jan, "will prove my story perfectly."

"How is this?" said the judge. "My dear fellow, this form is signed. And besides, it is almost time for lunch."

"I demand that you have that jar brought here," said Jan.

"Now, now," said Shannon soothingly. "He's a little violent at times, judge and—"

"I know," said the judge, nodding. Again he reached toward the button which would call a guard to take Jan away. It seemed that even then the sanitarium ambulance was outside and waiting.

There was the sound as of a chair being shoved determinedly back. Alice Hall eyed the judge with disapproval. "Your honor, the papers would like to print a story to the effect that you might have received money to put a millionaire in jail."

It was a terrible chance she was taking, Jan knew. And while he feared for her, his heart warmed toward her more than ever before.

"What's this?" cried the judge at the wholly unjust charge. "Are you mad?"

"Not at all," said Alice. "And I wonder if he is, either. His mistake lies in having been meek to a crowd of wolves. The papers, I think, would enjoy such a story, true or not. If it is even whispered about that Jan Palmer, heir to the Palmer interests, was railroaded to an insane asylum to cover up the thefts of his manager, Nathaniel Green—"

"What's this?" shouted Green. "Young lady, you are fired! Leave this office instantly."

"I may be fired but I shall not leave. Your honor," said Alice, crisply, "if Jan Palmer wants a copper jar brought here, perhaps it would be wise to bring that copper jar."

"I . . . uh . . . see your point," said the judge. "*O'Hoolihan!*"

In an hour the morosely lunchless judge was sitting in sad contemplation of the copper jar while Green walked in circles and said, "Nonsense, nonsense, nonsense! I'm due at the office this minute!"

"And so," said the judge, "this is the jar out of which the Ifrit came."

"Yes," said Jan, stepping up to it and lifting the leaden stopper.

"And how tall is an Ifrit?" said the judge.

"Fifteen feet," said Jan promptly. "But in another world they do not seem so tall—either that or we are larger."

"Fifteen feet?" said the judge. "And the jar is but four feet. My dear young man, I fail to see—"

The psychiatrist tittered, and the judge was suddenly pleased with himself.

"Well," said the judge, "that is that. It proves nothing except the charges already brought. The justness of them is plain to see."

Alice's face fell. She had wagered her job and lost, but her sympathy and attention were all for Jan.

In a very quiet voice Jan said, "Your honor, if I were you I would think twice before I call proof disproof. I might go as far as to say that it is dangerous for you to do so."

"A threat?" said the judge.

"Now, now, Jan," said Aunt Ethel. "He is *so* violent at times, your honor—"

"Aye, proof!" said Jan. "And a threat as well. A threat which I am quite capable of carrying out. There is one phrase of this story which I have yet to mention. It is the answer to the ancient problem of the wandering sleep soul. And so, one and all—" He took a firm grip upon the leaden stopper, his palm pressing hard against the imprinted Seal. "And so you are brought to this.

"By the Seal of Sulayman and by the token of all

the deeds already done by its mighty power, I invoke upon all of you, the sentence of Eternal Wakefulness!"

The psychiatrist tittered in the quiet room, and the others gathered heart. As nothing had happened, they were sure nothing would happen.

"The ambulance is waiting," said the judge. "O'Hoolihan, escort the young man out."

Jan stopped beside Alice. "Don't worry. Things may yet turn out well." He did not miss the moistness in her eyes, and he knew then that even though he might be mad, she loved him.

FIFTEEN

At dawn the sound of ten thousand kettledrums struck violently and shook the seventy-four from stem to taff!

Directly under the starboard gun deck, Jan leaped up, not yet awake but already aching from the concussion.

"Sit down!" barked the third sentry of the night, gesturing with the pistol.

Jan stared at the muzzle and then at the seaman's pale face and obediently seated himself upon the edge of the berth.

There came the groan of shifting yards and the pop of fluttering canvas as the seventy-four came about to bring her port batteries to bear. She heeled under the buffeting wind and began to pitch as she picked up speed. Pipes shrilled and bare feet slapped over planking and then the whole vessel leaped as the demi-cannon blasted away.

"What time is it?" said Jan.

"About six-thirty. Now pipe down. I'm sorry but I'm not supposed to talk to you."

"That's fine by me," said Jan.

A shriek of hurtling round shot pierced the air and a series of muffled thuds reported that the seventy-four had been hulled. But again yards creaked and canvas thundered. Again she came about and heeled. The recharged starboard batteries brayed flame and shot.

The sentry glanced up at the deck and nervously

wet his lips. Screaming grape-shot slapped like giant hailstones in the rigging and he flinched.

"You're lucky," said Jan. "If we're sunk, you get a nice clean burial. All in one piece."

"Shut up!"

"Well, isn't that better than being drowned *and* lacking arms and maybe legs? Listen to that musketry. We must be closing in on Zongri's fleet."

A broadside of their own was instantly answered by the roar of another close by. The seventy-four reeled, hesitated and then picked up again.

"Is that water I hear?" said Jan.

"Water? *Where?*"

"Hulled, probably. Many more like that and we'll get it before the rest of them up there. Still, I don't mind it. If a man is going to die, he might as well have some privacy."

"Stop it!"

"Why, that doesn't bother you, does it? Maybe you'd rather be blown up than merely sunk. And the sharks won't be able to get at you in here."

There is nothing worse than a dark hold when a battle rages, listening to the broadsides thunder and feeling the seventy-four trip and wallow as round shot took its count, hearing wounded scream and weep, sensing the rising levels in the bilges and having no idea whatever of how the battle goes. Men prefer dying where they can see the sun.

For an hour the din was incessant, and for an hour Jan remarked upon each expert broadside which was poured into them.

"The way she's listing now," said Jan. "We've probably lost a mast and they're too busy to cut it away. That cuts down the speed, you know, and makes it very easy for us to be boarded. Wasn't your relief supposed to be here by now?"

"Never mind my relief!"

"Ah, there's to be much weeping in Tarbuton this night for our brave lads. And weeping too in another world where men are nervous beyond account as they slumber. And how many will be the obituaries in the morning paper? Accidents, heart failure, murder. By the way, you haven't any people, I trust?"

"I have my mother!"

"And a girl too, I suppose. She's probably down at the wharves now, straining her eyes to sea in the hope of seeing the red banner returning. But, from the way that water rushes under us, I think she looks in vain. Personally, it's nothing to me. Returned I'd be executed. It matters very little how a man dies just as long as he is in one piece. This is a nice place now. The water is coming up under us at a very fast rate. We're hulled between wind and water and higher too, I'll wager. And as she lowers herself in the sea, more water will pour in—"

Round shot splintered a timber over their heads and the guard ducked to rise an instant later and steady his pistol, looking ashamed.

"Stop it!" grated the sentry. "When water comes over this deck, there's time enough to worry about that."

"Ah, but I was just about to tell you that water is already seeping over it from under this bunk. See?" And he pointed to a trail of oozing slime, the scum of the bilges carried seven feet above their safe level. "We're sinking," he said quietly.

But the sentry stood firm. The fury of the fight was deafening and the sound of activity on their own decks gave him heart. He twitched as spars crashed down over them, one end protruding through the gun deck. It had dropped through the hatch.

"Do you smell smoke?" said Jan.

"How could there help but be smoke?" challenged the sentry.

"Wood smoke, I mean. And what is that crackle?"

"Muskets, you fool."

"But you're testing the air. We're on fire and that means we'll have to come to grips with another ship.

. . . There! You heard that? Irons! There they go again! We're locked to another ship!"

The sentry heard hull grating against hull and the savage yells of sailors as they swept over the rails. Cutlasses crashed and pistols barked.

The sentry was uneasy. If they were swept from their own decks the ship would be deserted, abandoned to burn and sink. But he steadied the pistol in his hand and watched Tiger.

The tide of the hand fighting crashed back and forth over the heads, now in the stern, now in the waist. The smell of smoke thickened even in the double bottoms.

"Hear that rattle?" We're locked port and starboard to Barbossi vessels now. That's the end of us."

And indeed the yells did redouble and the decks sagged under the crushing weight of men. The violence of this finishing fight ate into the sentry's nerves. The water was almost to his knees now and the rush of it back and forth as they rolled in the trough made it hard for him to stand.

A blasting smash close at hand almost knocked the sentry down.

"Hulled!" cried Jan. "Hulled from the range of a foot!"

The water was roaring into the ship now and the sentry could not stand at all. Suddenly his nerves gave way. He wheeled, forgetting his prisoner, and vaulted up the ladder to the open air.

Jan shouted with relief. He slapped his hand over the Seal and cried, "Open wide!"

The brig door was shattered on its hinges. He rushed through it and dashed up the ladder which led to the gun deck. The planking was slippery with blood and he had to leap to clear piles of dead and dying behind the gun carriages. A square of blue showed over his head and he swarmed up the ladder to the quarterdeck.

Two sailors wearing the badge of the clenched talons were at the top. They faced him and their stained cutlasses swept back. Jan saw an officer stretched in death across the companionway mat. He ducked and snatched up the sword, flashing it erect to parry the downcoming slashes. He pressed back their steel and gained the deck.

All was carnage about him and the once trim vessel was but a sinking hull, held up now only by the grapnels of the two Barbossi vessels on either side. But Jan had no time to consider the situation. A third sailor had joined the two and the three cut at him from as many sides. He skipped backward to put his shoulders against the taffrail. He caught a glimpse of the last of the seventy-four's sailors fighting against the house and thought he saw the glint of blue there, showing that one or two officers were yet alive.

The officer's sword, a rapier half again as long as a cutlass, flicked like the tongue of a snake and kept them at bay, no matter how hard they strove to smash it down and so, breaking it, close in to the kill.

A flag was caught by Jan's eye. The vessel on their starboard was a flagship! Zongri's vessel! And that towering Ifrit who waded forward to help finish off the last of the seventy-four's crew was Zongri!

Jan redoubled his efforts and, leaving off mere guarding, began to attack on his own. The long steel flashed and laid open a sailor from shoulder to belt but the pain of it only brought the man on with fury.

Slowly, Jan was working himself along the rail, approaching the ratlines of the mizzen. His swift wrist worked tirelessly and finally, ripping under a cutlass, dashed in and came out dripping.

"Two!" exulted Tiger. "Come on! You can't live forever! Come on, I say! I want you!"

The rapier licked over one of the sailor's hilts.

"One!" cried Jan. "One! Come on!"

But the fellow had enough and rushed away. Jan flung himself up into the rigging, swarming to the crosstrees. So great was the vessel's list that he was out over the deck of the Barbossi flagship.

Before him spread the battle, covering half a dozen square miles of blue water. White smoke drifted like scud clouds everywhere, but the cannonading was done. Somehow Tarbuton had gotten eight ships into commission and had reinforced these with merchant vessels. But now the superior number of the Barbossi—pirates, they were, at best—had locked all but three Tarbuton men-o'-war in iron grips. The three were far off, already hull-down, fleeing for their lives with a score of Barbossis in pursuit.

Jan took a deep breath, not knowing whether he could meet with success or not.

He wrapped an arm about a halyard and gripped the ring. "By the Seal of Sulayman," he roared, "I command the sundering of every bolt and lock in these two Barbossi ships below!"

He reeled from the jerk he received. The grapnels which held so tight to the railings went abruptly limp, their splicing unwound. And then, slowly, the two Barbossi men-o'-war began to fall apart! Plank by plank they disintegrated, but all at once so that, within a minute or two, they were nothing but floating wood upon the water, all snarled in hemp and canvas through which struggled hundreds of men, screaming with terror as they fought toward the maimed seventy-four.

The knot of fighters on the quarterdeck below drew back, staring at the wreckage. For a moment friend and foe were side by side without offering a single blow.

Already four Barbossi men, two on each ratline and others waiting to step up, were intent upon Jan in the rigging.

Jan looked down, seeing cutlasses flashing in their teeth as they paused to wonder and shudder at the wreckage of their own.

Zongri had leaped back from the fray, his massive

torso red with blood, his face blacker than ever with the grime of smoke. And now he seemed to rise two feet in stature.

"The Seal!" he bellowed. "Who—"

He looked aloft. The Seal's flashing in the sunlight was not easy to miss. And Zongri saw something more. He sprang to the ratlines, knocking his own men aside, and raced up, roaring: "*You!* By Rani, today you die!"

"Rani is dead!" Tiger mocked him from above, tightening his hold on the rapier. "Last night she died in a heap of rubbish just as I shall kill you!"

Zongri was losing no time. His fangs were agleam and his eyes had lightning in them. His red hands shook the rigging and the very mizzenmast.

"By the Seal of Sulayman!" cried Jan. "I demand that every bolt in every Barbossi—"

Slash! Zongri's great saber passed within an inch of Jan's feet.

Jan's rapier licked out and stung the Ifrit, and then Jan raced up the mizzentopmast.

"I command," he roared, "that every Barbossi vessel be treated as these two!"

He had no time to witness the caving in of the fleet. Zongri was reaching for his boots, but far off he heard the terrified screams of the Barbossi pirates and the splash of masts dropping into the sea.

"Are you satisfied?" cried Jan. "Down or I'll burst this very ship apart under us!"

"I'll have your heart!" roared Zongri. And the topmast quivered underneath their climbing weights.

Jan got to the topgallant and paused for an instant. "You fool! You're done! Your fleet is gone and you've lost!"

"I'll have your life!" screamed Zongri, mounting still.

The wind had drifted the Tarbuton seventy-four away from the floating wreckage. The list was so bad that no man could have climbed the down side of the shrouds.

Jan took one last look at Zongri and then at the sea. He had to dive. But a hundred feet down made him wince.

"By the Seal of Sulayman" he shouted, kicking off Zongri's reaching grasp. And then, in a long dive, Jan left the mast. Even before he started to go he had begun it and it was scarcely out of his mouth before he hit the water. "Out with the mast!"

Green raced by him and he struggled to stop his descent. He fought his way upward again, swimming hard all the while to get as far from the ship as possible. Concussion hit him before he reached the top again and when he came spluttering and blowing to the surface he saw that the seventy-four had no mizzen.

He tried to raise himself in the sea but a wave did that for him, and he saw the mast, all tangled, floating some distance away.

Zongri, naturally, had been unable to clear himself of the rigging and, with it looped all around him, he fought hard to stay up, stunned and bleeding from the concussion.

Jan struck out swiftly for the seventy-four. There were halyards trailing, now that the mizzen had dropped, and he snatched one and pulled himself up it.

Almost against his head a serpentine thundered. He ducked and then bobbed up again to leap over the rail.

A strange sight met his eyes. Wounded and beaten into hiding, the seventy-four's crew, a full three quarters of which remained, were massed upon the quarterdeck and still they came out of the hatchways. In the waist of the ship Barbossis, weaponless now except for what they could pick up on the frigate, were trying to organize for a rush.

The three stern chasers and the serpentines were being loaded again in great haste and others were being lifted up through the after deck to reinforce the battery.

Flame and thunder and smoke rolled down like a blanket over the attackers in the waist, and when it cleared there were furrows plowed through them. But the Barbossi men had not given in. They were finding muskets and cutlasses and hurriedly forming, their front ranks already beating at the men on the raised quarter-deck.

"By the Seal of Sulayman," cried Jan, "I order that every weapon in Barbossi hands fall apart!"

Astounded, the seventy-four's gunners stopped at their loading to stare down into the waist where equally astounded sailors were hastily trying to fit blades to hilts and barrels to stocks. And even when they picked up whole ones from the deck, *they* came apart.

"Surrender," roared Jan, "or be shot down where you stand!"

It did not take them long, confronted with battery and small arms on the quarterdeck, to make up their minds. They threw down the useless segments of weapons and a deafening cheer resounded from the quarterdeck.

Jan turned to see two hairy, clawed hands wrapped about the rail. Zongri, bleeding and soggy, mounted. But he had no more than set his foot on the deck than twenty muskets were at his breast.

"Chain him," said Jan. "We'll take him as a trophy to Tarbuton!"

A growling voice beat upon Jan's ears. "What's this? What's this?" said Tyronin. "Who issues orders here? *Tiger!* Why, you—"

"Aye, Tiger!" said Jan. "And I'll be issuing orders for many a day to come. Get these decks cleared of prisoners. Put them under hatches and pick up those afloat on wreckage. Assemble your fleet and with all speed make way for Tarbuton!"

The audacity of it made Tyronin reel. He was about to bluster but Jan cut him impatiently short.

"I want no trouble from you. This is the last time I'll remind you, but I've no use for an ingrate. Get busy!"

The men, beginning to understand now what had happened, their eyes fixed upon the flashing Seal on Jan's wrist but also appreciating how he stood there, battle-grimed and terrifying, raised another cheer.

Tyronin was stupefied by it. He looked slowly all about him and then, seeing light, nodded briskly and set to work.

Hakon, severely cut up, had energy enough to touch Jan's hand.

"I knew, Tiger. Some day this had to happen. God bless you, my friend."

Tiger smiled back at him and then strode toward the companionway in search of Alice.

SIXTEEN

Late that afternoon, the huge black doors of the palace were thrown wide to admit the triumphal procession which now left the city hoarse with cheering behind them.

The officers of the shattered fleet were bunched together, sullen or hopeless or defiant, and many of their looks were reserved for Zongri, who marched quite alone, almost sinking under the weight of his irons—Zongri who had come back to again take up his rule and lead them swiftly to appalling defeat.

Behind the captives were borne several figureheads salvaged from the vanquished ships; gaudy things of frightful mien which glowered now all in vain.

The hall resounded to the echoes of the marching feet and the assembled army officers, half of them glad and the other half sad about the navy's victory, sent up a great shout when roaring drums and screaming horns heralded the approach of the victors. No news as yet had reached the palace beyond the tidings that the fleet returned victorious and so it was that Ramus sat up like a giant poker in her throne and wiped her disk eyes and blinked very hard. And so did every courtier and secretary and officer blink.

For in the van was a great chair of gold—Tyronin's personal chair, reserved always for the lord high admiral—and in that chair sat two human beings! It was so great a shock that the queen was heard to gasp. A slave—no, two slaves, and one robed as a temple dancer!—riding in such state?

And what was this? Behind them trooped Tyronin and all his captains, perfectly willing, even anxious, to cheer their leader onward!

"By the blood of Ba!!" croaked the queen. "What insanity is this? *Tiger!*"

The chair stopped before the throne with all the horde of high officials grouped about and Jan stepped down. He was grimed and tattered but the radiance of his handsome face made up for all the rest of it. He helped the dancing girl to the floor.

Alice, told time and again on the voyage in, that such was such and this was that, still could not realize it. Later the dancing girl would gradually take a part of her personality and so brighten it. But now she was dazzled by the jewels and silks and still unable to believe that this handsome devil who was but yet was not Jan Palmer, had the upper hand amidst these frightful people.

"*Tiger!*" cried Ramus again. "By the death of the devil, man, what's this?"

"Your majesty," said Tiger, bowing perfunctorily, "I give you Zongri again, and I give you the prisoners of a shattered fleet. The pirate might of Barbossi is no more."

"Admiral Tyronin!" thundered Ramus. "However this miracle came about is less amazing than why you allow a human—albeit Tiger—to occupy your place—"

But Tyronin indicated Tiger and said no more.

"Your majesty, last night I thieved a dancing girl from the Temple of Rani"—there was a sharp gasp—"and, unfortunately, caused a goddess of granite to be destroyed. I see there on your right a high priest. He has business with me?"

The high priest stepped angrily forward, purple at the confession. "Chattering ape of a human, you have the face to confess that you—"

"Hush," said Jan. "Commander Hakon, have the fool removed."

The high priest was removed and half a dozen other

priests took heed and made a great show of getting out of the hall. The army, knowing not which side to take, took none for the moment.

"Your rule has not been onerous to this land," said Jan. "Pray retain the throne. I care not for its worries."

"You . . . uh . . . what?" cried Ramus.

"Unless, of course," said Jan, "you want every human being in this world to awake this instant and so swarm over you and put you down! I dislike threats." But he touched the glittering Seal upon his hand and all saw it and recognized it. In that instant the army set up a great shout for Tiger and almost brought the roof down on their heads.

"Your majesty," said Tyronin, "have no fear of this man. Single-handed he routed the enemy and he has convinced me that he intends no ill."

Indeed, she could have done nothing about it. Alice felt the shock of her eyes and moved nearer to Jan, holding his arm tightly. He touched her hand reassuringly.

"You . . . you leave me the throne?" said Ramus.

"Aye," said Jan. "It is yours."

Ramus covered up by instantly getting busy. She roared out for the guards to take the Barbossi prisoners and strike off their heads. But Jan, marching up boldly between the two lions from which Alice dodged, shook his head.

"They'll cause no more trouble," he said. "In them you have the nucleus of your new fleet." He had come up to her right and leaned against the arm of her throne. "Zongri, now, that's a different matter."

"You said I was to rule."

"But not against my wishes," said Jan gently. "I advise that you sentence Zongri to ten thousand years of very hard labor and so have done with him."

Ramus sighed quiveringly and did as she was ordered.

Zongri was led beaten away, and he had no more than gone when a squad of men in naval uniform dashed in at the door, saw Jan up beside the throne and approached. In their midst they had two of Dauda's jackals and they were a very astonished pair. They quaked with terror as they gazed all about them at this unknown population.

They saw Alice and recognized her with a start. They looked closely at the tall man beside her and, after a moment, recognized a man who might have been Jan Palmer, but wasn't the Jan Palmer they had known.

An instant later another naval patrol came in from another way, dragging a fishmonger's wife who was all covered with dungeon straw. The young Ifrit lieutenant came to a smart stop and addressed Jan. "Sir, we found this one and yet another who was arrested but this morning by orders of the queen. They both profess to know nothing of this world and so we presume they are the people you require."

"Ah, yes," said Ramus. "I did have brought to me such another one. By Bal, Tiger, have you sentenced all these people? But what's to be done if they scatter about?"

"I myself can keep the secret. This lady with me has hers safe enough. And as for these others—" He paused and eyed the sorrowful lot. Shannon, Nathaniel Green and the judge of the court which had passed judgment upon him.

"Spare us!" wept Shannon. "We meant no harm to you! We are almost mad with finding ourselves where we are. What insanity—"

"Speak not of insanity," said Jan, wincing. "You will find yourselves in the land where your soul goes in sleep. Later you will remember that you have been fishmonger's wife and thieves. Just now you are brought before Ranus, who holds over you the power of death."

Ramus looked at Tiger and there was a certain shine in her eye which Alice did not at all like.

"Her majesty," said Tiger, "might be persuaded to

spare your lives and merely imprison you if you undo a great wrong in another world."

Aunt Ethel wept and wrung her filthy hands. Green shivered like a tree in a hurricane. And the sweat rolled from Shannon like lard.

"Your honor the judge," said Tiger, "these men and this woman have lied to you and so, in that other world, have done away with me. You can expect execution here if restitution is not made there. Am I making myself clear?"

"Oh, indeed, indeed!" wailed the judge.

"Very well," said Tiger. "Then you will be imprisoned here and not killed. Clear them out, lieutenant, and post reliable Marids over them. I have done."

Ramus looked at him and sighed. "You . . . you vanquished them single-handed, Tiger? Ah, God, but I always knew you had it in you. Pity me for having to abuse you so for what I thought was the good of my realm." She touched his hand and then faced her chamberlain. "Have the entire apartments of the left wing furnished for his lordship, Baron Tiger!" She looked at Alice and smiled sweetly. "My dear, have no fear of us. So long as you hold your secret, no jinni will ever raise his hand against you. Lord Boli, you fat fool! Get into town and buy a hundred serving wenches for her ladyship. Swiftly now and get rid of some of your fat!"

Tiger marched his bride-to-be down the steps. There was no ill will anywhere about him now. It had been spread about what the high priests of Rani had meant to do and how Rani herself had gotten her just deserts. And but for Tiger the town would even now be sacked and raped and in flames at the hands of Zongri's pirates. And so two army majors instantly elected themselves as escort and pushed others courteously aside, and with the blue of the royal navy preceding them, the party marched toward the apartments in preparation.

Alice was beginning to lose some of her fear. She looked searchingly at Jan's face and then squeezed his arm.

"Then it's true," she whispered. "It's true, it's true, it's true!"

And Jan gave her Tiger's swaggering smile and, content, she walked proudly beside him, returning the bows of the multitude through which they passed.

EPILOGUE

BACK ON EARTH, a few days later, an item ran in a Seattle paper.

EMBEZZLER COMMITS SUICIDE

Millionaire Heir Finds Losses

Nathaniel Green Leaves Confession
Note on Deathbed

SEATTLE, WASH. —. Nathaniel Green, long known in local shipping circles as manager of the Bering Steamship Corporation, committed suicide last night at his home on Queen Anne Hill.

Jan Palmer, recently absolved from the slaying of Professor Frobish, told police that even after he had noted the missing amounts he had not seen fit to bring charges, but, rather, had been on the point of discharging Green.

"It was not from any merciful intent," said Palmer at his home last night, "for the company was almost ruined. But I did not wish to mar my honeymoon or worry my bride."

This aftermath of the strange case of Professor Frobish climaxed the most publicized affair of the year. Green, who was mainly responsible for Palmer's false imprisonment in a local asylum, had evidently sought to cover up his embezzled funds by murdering Professor Frobish and thereby throwing the stigma of the crime upon the young millionaire. Though Judge Dougherty says this is probably the case, no post-mortem action is to be taken against Green and so the matter has been closed.